HONEY BEAR COSY MYSTERIES

HONEY BEE MURDER

DAHLIA DONOVAN

HOT TREE PUBLISHING

The Grasmere Cottage Mystery Trilogy

Dead in the Garden | Dead in the Pond | Dead in the Shop

Motts Cold Case Mystery Series

Poisoned Primrose | Pierced Peony | Pickled Petunia | Purloined Poinsettia

London Podcast Mystery Series

Cosplay Killer | Ghost Light Killer | Crown Court Killer

Honey Bear Cosy Mysteries

Honey Mead Murder | Honey Bee Murder | Honey Moon Murder

Stand-alone Romances

After the Scrum | At War With A Broken Heart | Forged in Flood | Found You | One Last Heist | Pure Dumb Luck | Here Comes The Son | All Lathered Up | Not Even A Mouse | Farm to Fabre | The Misguided Confession | Stubbed Toes & Dating Woes

The Sin Bin (Complete Series)

The Wanderer | The Caretaker | The Royal Marine | The Botanist | The Unexpected Santa | The Lion Tamer | Haka Ever After

HONEY BEE MURDER

HONEY BEAR MURDER MYSTERIES
BOOK 2

DAHLIA DONOVAN

TANGLED TREE PUBLISHING

For information, contact the publisher, Tangled Tree Publishing.

WWW.TANGLEDTREEPUBLISHING.COM

EDITING: Hot Tree Editing

COVER DESIGNER: BookSmith Design

E-BOOK ISBN: 978-1-922679-70-3

PAPAERBACK ISBN: 978-1-922679-71-0

For Bacon, who inspired every pet I've ever written into a novel.

ONE

GEORGE

"Control your sodding bees."

"Pardon?" George lifted his head from where he'd been inspecting one of the hives. He frowned at the man clothed from head to toe in what looked like a mosquito net used in camping. His hands were covered in thick winter gloves. "Aren't you boiling?"

"Control your sodding bees. I'm allergic."

The slight hint of an accent gave George a clue to the man's identity. He heard from his cousin Margo about the new neighbour. A wealthy entrepreneur who'd come up from London with friends. According to local gossip, they intended to open a business of some sort.

Gossip in their little village tended to be frequent and only partially accurate. However, it did

make for amusing and confusing moments. George had once heard a rumour about himself that he'd left a wife in Edinburgh when he'd moved to Dufftown, odd considering he preferred men—and had never been married.

"Are you daft? I said control your bees." The man was a second away from stamping his foot in petulant anger like a wayward toddler.

"How? Why are you out in my garden if you're allergic?" George moved away from the hive. The constant buzzing made it hard for him to focus on the conversation. "I'm George Sheth. I live in the cottage just up the hill. This is all part of my property. You'd have climbed the stone wall to get here from yours."

"Your bees are in my garden." He stepped towards George, who held his smoker out in front of him as if it would protect him. "Stop them."

"First, how do you know they're my bees? I don't own *all* the bees in Dufftown. Or Scotland. There are bees in nature. Living wild outside of my purview. Second, how precisely am I supposed to control flying insects?"

"Control them. Or I will." He spun around and stormed off towards his cottage, leaving George staring after him.

What a lovely human being.

George turned back towards the hive that he'd been inspecting. "Well, wee buzzy bits, control yourselves."

The bees had no response. George chuckled to himself and gathered up his tools. He'd done all he could do for the moment; it was time to check on the rest of the garden.

His wild, secret garden. The grass was over-grown, owing to his not mowing it during the summer. The entire property was designed to provide for his precious bees.

It was his pride and joy. His passion project. He grimaced at the words his cousin Margo often used to describe it. *Passion project.* A less patronising description for his autistic hyper-fixation on bees and his garden than he'd heard from others over the years.

A winding path led up from the hives through the wildflowers on either side up to his small stone cottage. His garden had a carefully crafted wildness to it. Every single part of it was geared towards creating a healthy environment for pollinators.

"Hello." George smiled when Bumble, his elderly rescue pug, came trundling down the path towards him. He flopped beside George as though all his energy had been sapped out of him. He crouched down to pick him up. "Life getting to be too much for you? Let's go inside and have a drink."

Once inside the cottage, George set Bumble down to let him rush over to slurp up water. He carefully peeled off his beekeeping garb, then ran his fingers through his long black hair, pulling it back into a ponytail.

Along with his last name, George had inherited his father's thick, black hair and brown eyes. The ones his mother had always claimed made her fall in love with him so many years ago. It was sweet but also annoying when he'd heard the same story a million times.

The Sheths had moved from Udaipur to Edinburgh when his father was young. His parents had met at university. But his uncle had been the one to move to Dufftown; Dada Ji had found it a quieter place to raise his young daughter.

After moving from Edinburgh, George fully understood the attraction. He'd been in Dufftown for several years. His cousin Margo had helped him find the perfect cottage, and he felt more at home in the small village than he ever had in the larger city.

Bumble bumped against his leg, pulling him out of his thoughts. He grabbed a towel to gently wipe his pug's face. His poor wee elderly dog required a lot of extra care.

George had taken in several older pugs in the past ten years. He'd developed a close relationship with a rescue organisation. It was always more difficult to find homes for elderly dogs who needed more help. "What do you think, Bumble? Friend or foe?"

Bumble huffed at him.

"I agree. I think the neighbour's more foe than friend." George finished carefully cleaning the many wrinkles and folds on Bumble's face. "There you go. Were you sniffing the flowers again? You've got pollen all over you. You're not *actually* a bumblebee."

Setting Bumble back on the floor, George made his way into the kitchen and got the kettle going for tea. His parents had sent a care package of his favourite chai blends from their most recent trip to visit family.

George hated travelling long distances. Planes were loud and crowded. They smelled funny in a way that he couldn't put out of his mind.

And the sounds. So many of them. It was an overwhelming experience to get on a metal tube in the sky. So he tended to avoid it at all costs whenever possible.

The bubbling water in the kettle broke him out of his thoughts, which was probably a good thing. He poured it into the chai mix and gave it a quick stir. His attention was drawn to the window above the sink.

"Of all the...." George frowned at the familiar stranger stomping up the path through his garden. "What now?"

"Open up." The man pounded on the back door.

George wandered over with his hand already reaching for his phone to give Murphy a text. He thought he might need backup. And until someone got to know him, Murphy Baird could seem quite intimidating, not to him, especially considering they'd been friends for years and started dating recently. "What do you want?"

"Open up. There are bees out here."

"Yes, you're outside in a garden in summer. There are bees everywhere." George's gaze darted down to make sure the door was securely locked. "I'm not letting you in my cottage. I don't know you."

"Open the sodding door. They might sting me." He pounded on the glass repeatedly, making Bumble scramble across the room and hide underneath the coffee table. "We have to discuss the bee situation."

George wanted to close his eyes, put his headphones on and pretend his nightmare of a neighbour didn't exist. Unfortunately, he wasn't brilliant at dealing with confrontation. "No. You can whinge at me from out there. Besides, how have you come to complain at me when you're quite clearly trespassing in my back garden after you climbed the wall?"

While the unnamed neighbour ranted at him through the glass, George heard his front door opening. Margo joined him seconds later with a rolling pin in one hand and her little Chihuahua, Treacle, at her feet. He snorted in amusement when she brandished it.

"Why don't you bugger off?" She stepped between George and the door. "You don't waltz through someone's private garden and demand things. Honestly. We'll set the dogs on you."

"We will?" George muttered. "What are you even doing here?"

"Murphy called. And unlike us, your neighbour doesn't know they're harmless," Margo whispered in return. She waved the rolling pin again. "Now, what do you want?"

The man took a deep breath as if to start ranting.

"I'm not your mother. I will not listen to a tantrum from a grown adult. Either speak to us like you have some semblance of self-control or bugger off home." Margo folded her arms, tapping the baking pin against her bicep. She made an impressively intimidating figure for someone in an apron and covered in flour. "Well? Get on with it. I've honey and saffron shortbread cooling on the counter in my cottage."

He pulled himself up, squaring his shoulders and sneering at them. "I'm Hector Griffin."

"Good for you." George exchanged a bewildered and bemused glance with his cousin. The name meant nothing to either of them. "Solid name. Congrats to your parents for choosing it."

"I own the Griffin-Lee Logistics."

"Right. Brilliant. What's that?" George wasn't sure how any of it explained why the man was ranting in his garden.

"I... it doesn't matter. I'm highly allergic to bees. And your bees keep buzzing around the flowers in my garden." Hector Griffin seemed, once again, one step away from stamping his feet like a wayward toddler. "And I demand you stop them."

"I imagine there are bees of some variety in every garden across the county at this time of year. How precisely have you identified them as mine?" George was half-tempted to invite the man inside his cottage, if only to stop his bizarre dancing around. "They're not labelled. Or colour coded. I don't name them. I can't say, 'Oh, that's Bob there by your ear.' They're bees."

His words didn't seem to offer any comfort to Hector, who immediately began flailing about as if a bee was by his ear. George sighed deeply. He wanted the man to go away and leave him alone.

It had been a lovely morning thus far while George had taken care of the hives. He'd watered the plants where needed and pulled a few weeds. All of the relaxation had vanished, floating away on the chaotic hurricane-force winds of his new neighbour's drama.

"If you're so allergic to bees...." Margo trailed off. She set the rolling pin on the nearby bookshelf. "This is absolutely ridiculous. I'm going outside. I'm not talking through the door like you're a wayward salesperson who can't take no for an answer."

George considered the man for a moment. He finally reached out to unlock the door. "Come inside. I'll put tea on for us. And you can explain why you think I can control bees that may or may not be connected with my hives."

"I—"

"Tea, first." George didn't have the mental energy to cope with Hector Griffin's particular brand of privilege. He was a man who appeared to expect the world to simply adjust to his demands. "Lots of it."

By the time George had tea ready, Murphy had arrived. He'd obviously been preparing for the upcoming Highland Games. He was in shorts and an old rugby shirt that showed off his muscles and bulk.

"Morning. I brought a few breakfast pastries." Murphy managed to appear intimidating even when both Bumble and Treacle bounded over to him. "Hector Griffin."

"Baird."

George glanced in confusion at Margo. He didn't think he'd missed the undertones of the brief exchange. "You two know each other?"

"We're acquainted." Hector sneered.

TWO

MURPHY

"Don't take it personally. Hector tends to forget the world doesn't revolve around his wants and needs." Murphy had met the owners of Griffin-Lee Logistics at a Chamber of Commerce business conference. They'd been talking about moving their business into the area, which had excited a few people and worried others. "Maybe I should call my cousin Sarah. I doubt you'll have met her yet. She's a detective constable with the Major Investigations Team that covers Moray County."

"Not necessary if he'd just control the bees." Hector seemed stuck on repeating himself as if the issue was they hadn't heard him the first time. He'd been going on for over twenty minutes since Murphy arrived.

"I think it's time for you to go." Murphy deftly stepped over the two pups at his feet and used his body to back Hector out of the house. "Go home, Mr Griffin. And quit your wall climbing into other people's gardens."

"Well, I—" Hector had nothing further to say when Murphy glowered at him with his arms folded across his chest. "*Fine.* I'll be speaking with my solicitor."

"About bees?" Murphy didn't even bother to hide his laughter. "You realise how absolutely barmy you'll sound?"

With a huff of frustration, Hector stomped away. Murphy remained outside to watch until it was clear he wouldn't return. He glanced down when he felt a cold nose against his leg.

"Hello, Bumble." Murphy watched the pug trundle behind his tiny best friend of a chihuahua. The two little dogs returned to the cottage, likely to find one of the many blankets or beds to curl up together to sleep. He followed them inside. "Well, he was pleasant."

There was a moment of strained silence. George had his arms wrapped around himself. He seemed completely overwhelmed by what had just happened.

From Murphy's experience, it often took several minutes to hours for things to sink in for George. As a result, he tended not to react instantly. Margo seemed to be keeping an eye on her cousin as well.

"So, how are Graeme and Maisie?" Margo broke the tense silence with a completely random subject change.

There was a pause before they all broke into slightly hysterical laughter. George sat heavily on the arm of the couch. His smile was definitely a little forced.

"My brother and sister-in-law are preparing the pub for another mead tasting. We've got the caramelised honey batch that was flavoured with blackberries. She's going for an ancient Druid theme to go with the darker mead. So prepare yourselves." Murphy had told Maisie that there was to be absolutely no dry ice at this event. The last time she'd brought it in, someone had been murdered. He wasn't taking any chances. "Here's hoping this one isn't quite as dramatic as the last."

"How many times can a person be murdered in your pub?" Margo grinned when he sent her a horrified glance. "Statistically speaking, odds are it won't happen again."

"Don't jinx me. Let's try to avoid any encounters

with the police. I'm not sure Sarah's recovered from our last adventure." Murphy had received several lectures from his cousin about the recent murder at his pub.

It hadn't been his fault. He hadn't asked someone to murder their husband in the middle of a tasting event at his place. And he certainly hadn't anticipated being dragged into the investigation as the initial suspect.

All in all, it was an experience Murphy hoped never to have to repeat. The only good part of the entire debacle had been the change in his relationship with George. They'd quit dancing around each other and finally put their feelings on the table.

"Well, if you've got things managed, I think I'll head home." Margo lived down the lane from George's place. She picked up Treacle and said her goodbyes. "Try to keep those bees under control."

"Bugger off." George collapsed back onto the couch with a sigh. "Maybe buzz off is more accurate."

"I love you too." Margo waved to both of them before heading out.

"Have you eaten?"

"I was going to enjoy a late breakfast. More of brunch at this point." George closed his eyes. He brought his arms up and crossed them over his face. "Control my bees. Control. My. Bees. *Control* my bees."

"Don't think it matters where you put the emphasis. It won't make sense to you or anyone else who isn't a posh prick." Murphy watched him in concern for a few seconds. He knew George would have to allow the stress of the confrontation to bleed off him. "How about I fix us something to eat? Give you a second to recover."

"Control my bees," George said the phrase to himself repeatedly until the words seemed to blend into nonsense. "I don't understand."

"I'm not even bothering to try. It might break my brain." Murphy hadn't been impressed by his brief encounter with the man at the conference. Today had further cemented his dislike. "A simple breakfast sandwich work for you?"

"Bees."

"Taking that as a yes." Murphy moved into the kitchen. He chuckled when Bumble followed him. The pug immediately went to sit on the plush rug in the corner, one intended for that precise purpose. "All right. What've we got in the fridge this morning?"

There was silence for a while as Murphy inspected the fridge's contents. He found bacon, eggs, and cheese. A fresh loaf of bread sat on the counter, likely one brought over by Margo at some point; she tended to be generous with her bakes.

"Paddy."

"Yes?" He glanced over his shoulder to find George had shifted around to lie on the couch. "You all right?"

"Feel floaty."

"Adrenaline crash. You'll be all right. Going to fix you some tea with extra sugar." Murphy got the kettle going.

Murphy Baird had earned his nickname Paddington for several reasons, mostly his surname and his size. He was stocky. Muscled, though, he didn't put nearly as much effort into staying fit as he'd done in his twenties. Now he was content to be healthy, if a little softer around the middle, something George seemed to enjoy.

Cutting several slices of bread, Murphy made a square hole in each piece. He fried up a couple rashers of bacon and set them aside. Bumble was particularly interested in sampling it for quality control.

After melting butter in the pan, Murphy set the bread into it. He cracked an egg into the hole of each slice, waited for it to harden a little, then laid a rasher, a piece of cheese, and finally, the bread square on top, pressing it back into the empty space.

Murphy waited a moment before flipping each slice over. It was his favourite way to make a breakfast sandwich. He plated them up just as George joined him. "Tomato sauce, brown sauce, or nothing?"

"Nothing. Just pure, unadulterated eggs, cheese, and bacon." George stepped over. He hesitated for a moment before slipping his arms around Murphy. He laid his head against his chest. "Thank you."

"Anytime." Murphy rested his chin on the top of George's head, holding him tightly with one arm while he deftly slid the last sandwich from pan to plate with his other hand. He set it back on the hob while turning off the burner. "Nothing fancy, but with the homemade bread, it should be hearty and delicious."

"Much like you. Hearty and delicious." George attempted to smother his snicker against Murphy's chest without success. "Not sure where I was going with that."

"I'll take it as a compliment." Murphy used his hold on George to move them both to the little kitchen table. "You'll feel better with some food in you. Tea's probably ready. I added more honey than usual, but I imagine you could use the boost."

George lowered his arms slowly. He stayed beside Murphy briefly before slumping into one of the chairs. "What am I supposed to do about my new neighbour? He's climbed the wall into my garden twice. What happens if he winds up getting stung?"

"Not your fault."

"But how can I stop him?" George tapped his fingers agitatedly against the table. He clenched his hands into fists to break the repetition. "He'll be more of a nuisance to me than the bees are to him."

Murphy set the plates on the table. He grabbed both mugs of tea and took a seat beside George. "The best thing you can do is simply ignore him. He's invading your privacy, so I suppose you could call Sarah or one of the local constables. They'd give him a warning to keep out of your garden."

"I don't want to get him in trouble."

"How about I chat with Sarah and see what she thinks? Worst-case scenario, I can bring Graeme over so the three of us can make a bigger boundary between the properties." Murphy thought he might also need to put up cameras so they'd have proof. "We'll see what the lovely DCI Baird thinks of the situation."

"Glad I got most of my outdoor tasks done today. Not sure I'll have the courage to go out into the garden. He might pop out from behind a hedge or something." George took a massive bite of the sandwich and nodded. "When's your next tasting?"

"End of the week. Friday. So Maisie's got a few days left to work her magic." Murphy allowed his sister-in-law free rein over everything but the mead itself. She had an eye for turning them into really fantastic events. He hoped this one didn't involve a dead body. People might not want to come. "Fancy a date night tomorrow?"

"We had one last night. And we've had brunch with a side of posh wanker." George eyed the rest of his sandwich. He offered a genuine smile. "Not bored of me yet?"

"Never going to be boring around you, George."

"Right. Fine." George became even more intensely interested in his brunch. "Tomorrow's brilliant."

"How goes your vlogging?"

George groaned loudly and shoved the last of his sandwich into his mouth.

"That good?"

He took his time finishing chewing and chugging

down some tea. "Why did I think it was a good idea?"

"You're sharing your love of bees with the world." Murphy hadn't been sure of the idea when Teagan brought it up. They'd been convinced George would enjoy sharing his hives with the world at large. He wasn't so sure. "You can do it. There's no rush. You set the schedule."

"I enjoyed showing the hives. I've filmed hours of footage of bees, the garden, and all my equipment." George clung to his mug of tea, staring morosely into it. "I've no idea what to do with editing."

"Thought you were going to let Tea give you a hand?"

George shrugged.

Murphy reached across the table to lightly grasp George's forearm. He rubbed his thumb soothingly across his skin. "Teagan offered because they enjoy the creative process. No shame in admitting you don't know how to do something. They'd love to teach you. They do videos for their auntie's hair salon in the village."

"I'll text them."

Murphy gave his arm one final squeeze before pulling back. "They'll be thrilled. Teagan chatted my ear off yesterday about it, wondering if you would let them participate in your project."

"Okay." George sounded more confident in his response this time. He managed a tired grin. "Why are people so exhausting to deal with?"

"I ask myself the same thing every sodding day."

THREE

GEORGE

Once Murphy left for the brewery, George dragged himself into the little office he'd made in the small alcove off his bedroom. Not much of one. There was a desk by a window looking out into the garden. It was just large enough for a computer and his camera.

Opening his email, George stared at the one sitting in his drafts. It had been there for days. He read it over for the hundredth time before hitting Send.

He logically knew Teagan wouldn't mind the message. But he'd agonised over it for days. It was impossible to shake his anxiety over pressing Send.

George turned off his computer. Maybe not seeing the screen would help. He reached down to

give Bumble's head a gentle pat. "How about we go out into the garden? Hopefully, we'll be free from the posh toddler."

Bumble trundled along behind him while he made his way through the cottage. He grabbed his camera from the shelf by the back door. There was no harm in getting more footage.

His goal was to create a lovely, calm aesthetic for his videos. He did dispense some bee knowledge. But mostly, he wanted to share his joy in the world in a relaxing way. Teagan had promised there was an entire genre on YouTube that fit his niche.

Once the door was open, Bumble immediately rushed out to his favourite spot in the garden. He rolled around in the grass before plopping down on his belly. George made a mental note to ensure he got all the pollen off his pug later.

When the end of summer rolled around, George planned to clear out much of the flowers planted near the hives. He'd been talking to Murphy about what flavours he wanted to experiment with for his mead. One thing he wanted to put in was blackberry bushes around the hives.

They hoped it would add an interesting depth to the honey when combined with the other plants and flowers. Each year, George tried experimenting with a different set-up, particularly with those closest to the hives. It made subtle changes for Murphy to play with when making his mead.

George had no idea how Murphy and Teagan came up with their ideas. However, he enjoyed going to the brewery to watch them in action. It was like watching two slightly wild scientists at work.

Zooming out with the camera, George scanned the length of the garden. He followed the winding path through the taller patches of wildflowers. His entire goal had been to create the wildness of the outdoors in the confines of his home.

It was often like a storybook coming to life around him. The vines creeping up his little stone cottage helped with the imagery. A blanket of colours marked the path leading down a hill to the small meadow with his hives.

Stone walls cordoned off the property. Hedges and ancient trees filled in gaps where time had eroded the walls. It was magical and perfect, something George hoped to share with the world through his videos.

A growl from Bumble drew his attention. The pug was relatively mild-mannered. George had rarely heard him bark, let alone attempt to sound menacing.

As menacing as a small, wrinkled, old dog could be with his snuffling and trundling.

While George filmed, Bumble came over to sit beside him, still huffing and grumbling in the direction of the hives. His courage finally failed him. He decided they'd spend enough time outside for the moment.

Bumble refused to follow him, another strange sign. George retraced his steps and picked him up. He walked quickly, resisting the urge to peer over his shoulder every few seconds.

Someone or something had been out there. Bumble didn't growl at just anything. George hoped it was simply a stray dog or Hector stumbling around for whatever reason.

"Okay. What are we doing?" George locked the door.

It was boiling in the cottage. The weather had been exceptionally warm. George would usually open all the windows, allowing the lovely breeze to keep things cool.

But he didn't quite feel okay with having the cottage open. What if Hector showed back up to shout at him? He'd had more than enough confrontation for one day.

More than enough.

George set his camera to the side and went to find his phone. Unfortunately, it was buried under the blankets that Bumble had been fluffing for a nap. He grumped at being dislodged even for the briefest second. "My apologies. How terribly rough your life must be."

Sending a text to Margo to see if she was busy, George went into the kitchen and filled a cup from the kitchen tap. He watered all the various plants inside the cottage. There were bits of greenery all over the place.

Margo invited him over to spend the afternoon helping in her garden. She also reminded him of the impending visit from his dad, who planned to come for the Highland Games. His mum had intended to visit with friends elsewhere.

His dad didn't do well on his own and wanted to visit with George along with his brother and niece. It wasn't an unwelcome trip. But it would be the first since he'd begun dating Murphy.

How did he introduce an old friend as his boyfriend?

Boyfriend.

Is he my boyfriend?

It seemed like the wrong word for Murphy. *Partner? Spouse? Lover?* George could think of a hundred different labels, but none of them felt right. He'd stick with boyfriend to avoid confusing his dad.

They were definitely in a relationship, even if labels eluded him. George had always found it awkward to use them. Names were also something that had taken him an exceptionally long time to get used to using.

It made him uncomfortable, a quirk of being autistic but not the most difficult one. People rarely noticed when he didn't use their names as frequently as a non-autistic might. He tried to pick his battles when it came to pushing through his own discomfort.

"Want to go see Treacle?" George smiled when Bumble immediately perked up at the sound of his best friend's name. "Oh? For him, you'll happily move. I see where I stand. Come on, then. Let's go for a walk."

FOUR

MURPHY

"Bees."

"Yes, bees. Bzz. Buzzing. Bees. You heard me the first four times, Sarah." Murphy massaged his forehead and tried to ignore a snickering Teagan. He'd been on the phone with his detective constable cousin for ten minutes, attempting to explain the bizarre events at George's cottage. "Bees."

"He wanted George to control them."

"It won't make any more sense if you force me to repeat myself for a hundredth time." Murphy waved Teagan away. They'd already heard the story of what happened and been highly entertained. "I'm worried about George. What if this bloke hops the hedge again and decides to wreck the hives?"

"Then I imagine he's not long for this world if

he's truly allergic. Bees tend to sting." Sarah didn't seem to be overly concerned. "What do you want me to do? Caution him?"

"He trespassed twice, plus he threatened George."

"And if George makes a complaint, I'm sure one of the competent constables in the area will caution him. So what do you want me to do? Arrest him?" Sarah hung up a second later, still muttering about bees and daft cousins.

Murphy rolled his eyes at the phone. "Goodbye is always so hard for her."

Tossing his phone onto the table behind him, Murphy had a bad feeling about Hector Griffin. He hadn't liked how manic the man had seemed when ranting about bees. He and George had a disturbing number of close calls just a month prior, and he wasn't anxious to repeat the experience.

"Well?"

"You heard most of the conversation, Tea, the dropper of eaves." Murphy scratched absently at his beard. "I can't blame Sarah. What do they really have to go on? A magistrate would laugh them out of court if they even tried."

"Are you worried Griffin might escalate?"

"I can't shake the sense of impending doom."

"Maybe you just need a good trip to the loo?" Teagan ducked when a bag of lavender was tossed in their direction. "What?"

"How about we talk about our plans for the day?"

"Oh? Since you skipped the morning to engage in bee shenanigans and a romantic brunch with the adorable Captain Buzz?" Teagan had dyed their hair into a wild combination of reds and oranges. It made an apt representation of their bright spirit. He'd known their auntie from years and years ago when she'd moved from Jamaica. "We're testing one of the berry meads we bottled last month."

"Blackberry with caramelised honey?"

"That one. The strawberry honey one looks interesting as well, but not sure it's going to fit with the Druid theme. Maybe one of the herbal ones instead?" Teagan grabbed their mead journal. They kept detailed notes on recipes, successes, and failures. "We've got three or four that'll be ready in time."

"There's the lemon and ginger one. We have vanilla and lavender. There's the chilli-spiced one. There's enough to make for a dramatic Druid night." Murphy flipped through the pages, checking the pages for what they had available. "We'll do the caramelised honey with blackberry, cherry-chilli mead, and perhaps lemon and ginger if we need a third."

"I'll grab the sample bottles. We'll want to make sure they're ready." Teagan slid off the stool they'd been perched on before disappearing into the temperature-controlled room, where they stored all the mead.

One thing Murphy learned early on was to make separate smaller bottles of mead. It allowed them to taste a batch without opening one of the larger casks. He jotted a few notes in the journal while waiting for them to return.

"You get lost?" Murphy called out when they'd been gone for several minutes.

"Your sodding brother decided to do a spring clean in summer, so he's moved everything around." Teagan cursed Graeme out for a few seconds before giving a triumphant cheer. "Found the bottles. Why did you let him reorganise things?"

"It kept him busy."

"So, we're suffering because your brother was aggravating you?" Teagan glowered at him.

"Basically." Murphy flipped the mead journal to the page for the caramelised honey and blackberry. He tried to remember to jot things down as they went. His memory couldn't be trusted. "Here. I'll open the first one. Grab a couple of the tasting mugs?"

"On it." Teagan set the two bottles on the work-table in front of him. They went over to the shelf above the large sink, where they kept a variety of mismatched mugs. "Have you decided where you're taking George on your date night?"

"Date night in?"

"How many of those have you done?" Teagan poured a measure of the blackberry mead into the mugs. "I'm aware George doesn't always enjoy going to restaurants or other potentially crowded places. Maybe take him for a drive and have a picnic? Something other than cooking for each other at his cottage."

"It's a nice cottage," Murphy mumbled before sniffing the mead. "Take a whiff."

Teagan swirled the mead around and then sniffed it. "Oh, that's lovely. Put a few stars next to the recipe."

"Might want to give it a taste first. Might be utter shite while smelling *lovely*." Murphy had to admit, after taking a sip, it was, in fact, delightful. "Fine. Stars it is."

"Told you. The nose doesn't lie." Teagan tapped

their nose. They had a tiny taste and then chugged down the rest of the mead. "I could polish off the entire sodding bottle. Maybe we should do an entire collection with caramelised honey? Not just black-berry but other combinations."

It wasn't a bad idea. They'd done a few different blackberry meads in the past. However, the caramelised honey added more depth than Murphy had expected.

Grabbing the journal, Murphy jotted down their thoughts about the mead. He made sure to notate the date and time. Teagan reminded him to make a note in their ideas section about using caramelised honey more.

"You know, there's a restaurant next to my auntie's salon."

"I'm aware. A nice restaurant. We've eaten there probably a hundred times." Murphy was only slightly exaggerating.

"My point is I'm good friends with the manager. How about I see if they'll set up a little private space for the two of you? You can pretend you're being all romantic for an hour, then go home and play video games." Teagan rinsed out their mugs and brought them back for the second tasting. "Think about it.

They've a cosy little room off the main dining area. It'd be perfect for you both."

"Not too much?" Murphy tried to make things easier for George whenever possible without treating him like a child or taking decisions away from him. "I'll ask him. Can they do it on short notice?"

"For me?" They smiled brightly. "I'll text them once we're done with this."

"Thanks, Tea."

"I adore George. He's brilliant. Just don't want you mucking things up." Teagan winked when he grumbled at them. "Yes, yes, I'm aware of your general air of grumpiness, Paddington. Reel it back in. Maybe this cherry-chilli mead will spice up your mood."

"Does it need to be spiced up?" Murphy gave the mead a sniff. "Not as good as the blackberry. Though maybe that's a personal thing because I prefer it to cherry."

"Smells divine to me. I could bathe in this scent."

"Please don't." Murphy didn't necessarily do well with spice. They'd tried to carefully balance the chilli pepper with the honey in the hopes of creating a flavour everyone could enjoy. He hesitantly sipped the mead. "Oh."

"Oh? What does that mean?" Teagan gave into

their curiosity and drank theirs as well. "This settles it. We're doing an entire line of caramelised honey mead. Maybe we should do more with spices as well. This is spectacular."

"Perfect level of heat." Murphy returned to the journal, making sure to write down their thoughts on the recipe. "Not sure I'd change anything with what we've done aside from maybe allowing it to sit another week. Maybe. I think the flavour might develop even further with more time."

"We've got a few days before the event, so we can see if it makes a difference." Teagan sealed both bottles, setting them aside and taking the mugs over to rinse out. "I'll text my friend now and see if they can fit you and George in tomorrow night."

Nodding, Murphy decided not to fight Teagan on the subject. They could be stubborn when they had an idea. Instead, he went to find his phone and sent George a message to see if he was even interested in the concept. Murphy would have to upset Teagan's plans for them if he wasn't.

"Tea? I'm going to check in on Graeme and Maisie and see how the preparation is going." Murphy headed outside. He could easily have gone through the inner doors leading into the pub. He wanted to enjoy some fresh air.

The early sunshine had vanished. Grey clouds completely filled the sky. It had an ominously menacing feel to it.

Murphy shook his head, trying to brush off the sensation. *It's fine. Everything's going well. Stop borrowing trouble because we're in for rain.*

FIVE

GEORGE

"You can sleep here." Margo offered for the fourth time when George hovered by the front door, hesitating to actually step outside. "I don't mind."

"No, no, I can't do that. I'm overreacting." George pushed the door open and went outside. It was a lovely evening. The sun had set, but there was still plenty of light out. "Come on, Bumble."

Bumble appeared equally hesitant about leaving, though that was more to do with saying goodbye to Treacle. The two dogs adored each other. George thought they'd spend every waking hour together if allowed.

"You'll see Treacle another day." George gently nudged the pug forward on the path. He finally

began trundling along beside him with a little more enthusiasm. "There we go. Just you and I, along the lane."

It was completely irrational for his heart to start racing when they reached the cottage. Completely. Totally. Yet, George had to force himself to calm down. He wasn't afraid of being alone; he preferred it.

And he wasn't going to allow a posh toddler to ruin his cosy oasis for him.

"All right. Ready for your supper?" George quickly put together Bumble's evening meal, setting it down on the mat in the living room. Then, he grabbed the remote to turn on the telly. The sound helped drown out his thoughts, if nothing else. "Slow down. It's not going anywhere."

Bumble inhaled his food and stumbled into his pile of blankets. George gave him some time to nap. They could go for one last walk later.

Flipping through the channels, George finally gave up on finding something to hold his attention. His thoughts were all over the place. Confrontation always threw him off.

The worst part was that now it was all over, George could think of a million things he should've said to the man. His wittiest replies came long after a conversation was over. Being clever didn't matter if they were always a delayed reaction rather than an in-the-moment occurrence.

Turning off the telly, George decided to walk Bumble one last time in the garden. Of course, he wasn't pleased with being dragged out from his blankets. But he eventually meandered out the back door, grunting and grumbling the entire way.

To his relief, nothing seemed out of the ordinary from what George could see. He'd check on his hives in the morning. It might not be pitch-black outside, but he still had no intentions of wandering all the way down to bees at night, not with a neighbour prone to hopping the wall.

Bumble spent all of a few minutes trundling along in the grass. Finally, he trotted back into the cottage without glancing at George. His intentions to go to sleep were quite clear.

"All right, little old man. We'll get you all cosy in bed." George checked all the windows and doors, something he'd never done in the past. Hector Griffin had made him overly cautious. "Ready?"

The only answer from Bumble was a rumbling little snore. George chuckled. He carefully got Bumble comfortable in a mound of blankets on the bed before heading into the en suite for a quick shower.

After his shower, George had just changed into a fresh pair of shorts and a T-shirt when the doorbell rang. Bumble bolted up out of the blankets. "Easy there. Let's not go tumbling headfirst off the bed."

Setting Bumble on the floor, George made his way to the front door. He frowned when Sarah Baird and her fellow detective constable, Elwin Smith, greeted him grimly. A sinking feeling settled into his stomach.

"Is it Margo? Is she all right?"

"She's fine." Sarah was quick to reassure him. "Murphy mentioned you'd had trouble with your neighbour. Hector Griffin?"

"He had trouble with me. I only met him today when he trespassed into my garden twice to tell me to control my bees. He claimed they were going over into his property." George pressed his lips together, trying to stop himself from rambling on. He liked both of the detectives, but he was suddenly suspicious about their showing up so late at night. "What's going on? You haven't come to talk about him making a nuisance of himself, have you?"

"We haven't. He was found dead in his cottage this evening." Sarah got straight to the point. "Can you tell us where you were? Have you been home all night?"

"I was at Margo's for much of the afternoon and evening. Why?" George narrowed his eyes at the two of them. "I think I should give Evan Chan a call."

"We just have a few questions about your whereabouts this evening." Detective Constable Smith tried to set him at ease.

At least, George thought that was the point. He'd never been good at picking up on a person's tone of voice. It was one of the reasons why he wanted Evan there—someone to help him navigate questions in a system not built for dealing with the neurodivergent.

"I'm going to give Evan a call." George retraced his steps back to the living room to find his phone. He quickly dialled their solicitor friend, who answered on the fourth ring. "I need help."

Evan, to his credit, didn't even seem thrown by the request. "Where are you?"

"My cottage, at the moment. My neighbour was found dead."

"The new one? Terrified of bees?" Evan sounded more awake than he had a few seconds earlier. "Graeme mentioned someone had been harassing you. What's going on?"

"The police want to know where I was this evening."

"Don't say another word to them. I'm getting dressed. I'll be there as quickly as I can." Evan hung up before George could respond.

"Okay." George slowly lowered his phone and set it on the back of the couch. He traced the tattooed bees on his middle finger, something he often did to soothe himself in stressful situations. "Okay. I haven't done anything. It's going to be fine. Stay calm. Don't answer any questions. It's going to be fine."

The two detectives were still standing by his front door when George finally returned. He fidgeted under their intense stare. They threw a few questions at him, but he refused to say anything at all.

"George." Sarah massaged her forehead. "If you don't want to answer, you can at least say no comment. You don't have to quite literally go non-verbal."

He was saved from having to answer when a car pulled up behind the detectives' vehicle. Evan hopped out and practically jogged up the path to them. He dragged a hand through his still messy hair.

"How'd you get here so fast from Keith?" George muttered to Evan, who'd come to stand beside him.

"I wasn't in Keith," Evan whispered back.

George narrowed his eyes before grinning broadly. "Oh? Where were you? New date?"

"If the two of you wouldn't mind focusing for a second?" Elwin interrupted them before the conversation could go any further. "We need to know where George was this evening."

"Why?" Evan had positioned himself slightly in front of George, blocking him partly from view. "How did Mr...."

"Griffin." George leaned forward to whisper to him. "Hector Griffin. The one afraid of the bees."

"How did Mr Griffin die?" Evan had mastered the ability to maintain a straight face no matter the situation. "And how does it relate to my client?"

"Who?"

"You." Evan shushed George with a glance before returning his attention to the detectives. "You were quick to come here after Mr Griffin's death. Have you already determined the manner in which he passed?"

Elwin exchanged a look with his partner before answering the question. "Suspected anaphylactic shock. Our investigation is still in the early stages."

"And yet you found yourself here? Questioning my client?"

"We've only asked where he was. There's nothing sinister in the questions." Sarah tried to smooth things over before they could get confrontational. "We've made no assumptions."

"Anaphylactic shock would imply Mr Griffin's death was likely accidental. He claimed to be allergic to bees. I assume this led you to my client." Evan crossed his arms over his chest. "Are you suggesting George has trained his hives and sent them in as assassins? Do you understand how absolutely ludicrous the suggestion is? How defamatory?"

"We haven't made any such suggestion. All we've asked is where he spent the afternoon and evening." Elwin stepped into the conversation before his partner could respond. "We understand from one of Mr Griffin's friends that he'd confronted George earlier in the day about the bees."

"I can't control where bees go. There are more bees in Moray County than mine. How on earth could you possibly hope to differentiate?" George huffed into silence when Evan patted him on the arm. "I was at Margo's for most of the afternoon until about an hour ago."

"Enough. The police have no reason to question

you. I imagine Mr Griffin could easily have stumbled into a bee in his garden. One entirely unconnected to yours." Evan shifted so he was standing completely in front of George, blocking his view of the detectives. "Unless you have some evidence to the contrary?"

Sarah hesitated briefly before she decided to give them more information. "Mr Griffin was found dead inside his home by his boyfriend. All the windows and doors were locked. He had netting attached to every single one to prevent any flying insects from entering the cottage."

"And?" George held his hands up when Evan glared over his shoulder at him. "I don't see the... oh."

It occurred to George what the police had to consider. He had hives full of bees available to him. And he had a lot of experience in dealing with them. So theoretically, it would be relatively simple for him to capture a few and then release them into someone's cottage.

"Too impractical," George mumbled to himself.

"What is too impractical?" Elwin prompted when he didn't say anything else.

"My client is exercising his right to not say anything." Evan reached back to gently push George further into the cottage. "George. Back inside. They can request a more formal conversation if they have any further questions."

Wincing at the pinched expression on Sarah's face, George twisted around and made his way into the kitchen. A sleepy Bumble sat up briefly, then flumped into his blankets. He chuckled to himself as he began making tea for himself and Evan.

"I've sent a text message to the group chat." Evan strolled into the kitchen with his phone in hand. His fingers flew across the screen. "Murphy's on his way. Margo said she'd pop by in the morning, and I imagine Teagan will also join us soon since they were at your cousin's place."

"How'd you get here so fast?" George wasn't ready to discuss Hector and his untimely demise. "Were you in town?"

"George." Evan leaned against the kitchen counter across from him. "Why did you say it was impractical?"

"You can't exactly make bees do what you want. They're not going to immediately see a person and attack. They're not fluffy, flying assassins. So there's no way to guarantee they're going to sting someone." George snickered at the idea of little bumblebee ninjas. "I find it hard to believe it worked. I just... have questions."

They heard a knock on the door a few seconds later. George was surprised to find both of the detectives still there. He frowned at them.

"We need help dealing with the bees." Sarah got straight to the point. She nodded to Evan, who came up behind him. "No questions about the death. I promise. We've just got a cottage full of the stingy bastards, and I'm not anxious to get stung. Can you help?"

"Wait. The bees are alive?" George glanced at the police in confusion. "You haven't found any dead ones?"

"A couple stuck in the netting. But the rest appear to be alive." Elwin shrugged.

"Was there a dead bee on his body?" George was growing increasingly confused. "Anywhere near it?"

"We can't comment—"

"If you've found no dead bees on or around him, I've no idea how you think he was stung. It's not possible. They tend to die after they lose their stingers." George didn't think this was completely new information. "How do you even know that's how he died?"

SIX

MURPHY

On the drive to George's, Murphy spent much of his time cursing their luck. How had they wound up in two murder mysteries in the space of a month? It defied belief.

The text message from Evan had sent him scrambling out of bed. Murphy had known Hector Griffin was trouble. He didn't think a suspicious death would be the brand of a particular problem the man brought into their lives.

A host of worst-case scenarios flew through his mind on the drive down the lane to the cottage. Murphy was surprised to see Sarah's car still parked behind George's vehicle. Evan's was on the other side, so Murphy pulled up beside him.

"Paddy." Elwin acknowledged him with a nod.

"What's going on?" Murphy could see Evan and George speaking further into the cottage. Sarah stood nearby. "Are you guarding the door?"

"Trying to keep from crowding George." Elwin gave him a wry smile when they heard slightly raised voices. "Despite appearances, we're fond of Captain Buzz. He's a delight, and he's certainly made you less of a grump to deal with."

"Thanks." Murphy rolled his eyes at the detective constable he'd known for much of his life. "You can't seriously believe George killed anyone."

"What I believe and what I have to investigate are two very different animals, Paddy. And you know it. We haven't accused him of anything. All we know is the man had quite an intense confrontation with your boyfriend hours before he died." Elwin kept his voice low so they weren't heard inside the cottage. "Chan's a brilliant solicitor, but all we have are some simple questions so we can move on with our inquiry."

"I'm not pushing George to answer any questions without the presence of a solicitor." Murphy liked Elwin, and he loved his cousin Sarah dearly, but they were wrong on this point. "I had one—and he needs one even more."

As an autistic, George had an even higher

chance of being misunderstood or misunderstanding the questions. He could talk himself into trouble while being completely innocent. Murphy wouldn't let him get screwed over, even by those who had the best of intentions.

They went into the cottage, where Sarah was asking questions. Murphy leaned against the wall across from them. Evan was doing a brilliant job of carefully deflecting some of them.

"Did you notice anything strange this evening?" Sarah changed tactics.

George glanced at Evan first before answering. "No. Oh, wait, there was something. This afternoon, Bumble and I were in the garden when he started growling and barking. It was unusual for him. That's when I decided to spend the rest of the evening at Margo's."

"And you didn't see anyone?"

"Have you seen the height of my flowers? From where I stood, someone could've been by the hives, and I wouldn't have known aside from Bumble growling." George reached down to lift the pug up when he perked up at hearing his name. "I thought maybe Hector Griffin had come by for another confrontation over the bees, so I decided to go to Margo's."

"And you never went to his cottage?" Detective Constable Elwin prompted, likely sensing George might answer a few more questions. "At all?"

"I've been in the cottage once years ago when I was house hunting for my move. I've never been inside it again, and certainly not since his arrival." George cuddled Bumble against his chest and rested his chin on top of his head. "I had no interaction with him after our argument. Well, less of an argument and more of a tantrum on his part. I am not the pied piper of bees."

"Can I put that in my report?" Elwin grinned at Sarah, who heaved a tired sigh. "So, yes?"

"Off the record, I've never once believed you capable of hurting someone." Sarah ignored Elwin and Murphy when they continued to snicker about the pied piper of bees. She focused on George. "We have to ask questions. He apparently told his friend about the confrontation. It's the first thing they mentioned to us when we arrived at the scene."

"And you don't find *that* suspicious?" Evan stepped into the conversation again. He deftly manoeuvred himself in front of George, placing himself in front of his client. "It's always lovely to see you both, but I believe this questioning is over unless you want to make it official. In which case, I'll be representing my client when you put anything on the record."

"Evan." Sarah pursed her lips. She regained control of herself a second later. "We'll see ourselves out. Gentlemen. Murphy."

"Oh. Harsh. And unnecessary. I'm as much of a gentleman as these two." Murphy allowed the slight dig, knowing Sarah was attempting to lighten the mood. "I'll walk you out."

Following the two police through the cottage, Murphy heard Evan murmuring to George behind him. He hoped the solicitor was reassuring him. He had nothing to worry about.

"Sarah." Murphy waited until they'd gotten to her vehicle to speak. He didn't want to risk George overhearing. "You can't possibly think he'd do this. But, if nothing else, he'd never hurt his bees. Likes them more than people."

"I can't say that I blame him." Elwin held his hands up when Sarah glowered at him. "Can you?"

"Not helping, either of you." Sarah pinched the bridge of her nose. She stared off into the distance for a brief moment. "My job is to follow the evidence— personal feelings aside."

"I'm not trying to stop you from doing your job."

"Paddy." Sarah dropped her hand from her nose.

She eyed him suspiciously. "Stay out of the inquiry this time. You're not bloody Taggart, all right?"

"There has been a murder. Or a death. But given our luck, I'm guessing the former. I could be wrong." Murphy raised his hands in surrender. "Not planning to stick my nose into your business."

"Fine. We're going to swing back by Griffin's house. Once it's clear, we might need George to deal with the bees unless he can recommend someone else to give us a hand. Actually, it might be better for it to not be him." Sarah massaged her forehead. "Sodding flying insects. Stingy little bastards."

"If you clear out everyone else, you can escort George into the house to get the bees. Or... try opening all the windows and doors." Murphy ignored the deepening of her scowl. "I'm trying to help."

His cousin didn't seem to believe him, but she did get into her vehicle and slam the door. Elwin gave him a friendly wave and joined her. Murphy watched until their lights were out of sight.

He couldn't blame Sarah for her annoyance. It had been barely a month ago when Murphy had been the one accused of killing a man in his pub. They'd poked their nose into the inquiry when it appeared to have stalled.

Murphy called it helping. Sarah had used words like interfering and annoying. He loved his cousin like a sister, and their relationship was often more like siblings. *I'm not letting anyone even hint at George being involved.*

"Have they gone?" George joined him outside. "Evan's chattering away on the phone to Teagan. They'll bring something to eat since I doubt any of us are getting to sleep anytime soon."

"They have. They'll give us a call if assistance is needed to deal with the bees." Murphy slipped his arm around George's back, drawing him into his side. "Are you okay?"

"This how you felt after they questioned you?"

"Like a wrung-out towel?" Murphy rubbed his hand up and down George's arm. "We're not going to let anything happen to you. Evan's a bloody good solicitor. He'll keep you out of trouble if they have any more questions."

"I'd prefer to have answers for what happened." George leaned his head against Murphy's side. "I wonder who the friend is that told the police about the argument. And what exactly did they say?"

"Only one way to find out. We'll see if we can talk Teagan into paying a visit to offer their condolences. His friends obviously know who you are—

and probably me." Murphy knew they'd be up for it. "We'll need to ensure they don't take Evan with them. Someone might recognise him as my solicitor and, by extension yours."

They walked into the kitchen. With his arm still around George, they had to shift slightly to avoid knocking things over. The kettle had gone cold, so he reached over to switch it on again.

"About that date night out." George sounded utterly exhausted.

"Yeah?"

"How about we get a takeaway and eat in? There's a new documentary I've wanted to see, and going out sounds like more than I can handle." He'd practically wilted into Murphy's embrace. "Do you mind?"

"Spend a cosy evening in instead of dealing with the chaos of the general public?" Murphy pressed a kiss to the side of George's head. "Sounds absolutely perfect."

SEVEN

GEORGE

T H E   F O L L O W I N G   M O R N I N G   G E O R G E   W O K E   U P absolutely exhausted. It took several minutes of Bumble trampling over him before he sat up and turned off the alarm on his phone. He had no memory of hitting Snooze, but he'd done it multiple times.

Pulling on his robe, George wandered out into the garden with Bumble and down the path to check on his hives. Nothing seemed amiss with them, though he noticed a few areas where the grass appeared to be flattened. Had he done that?

Heading back to the cottage, George had barely enough time to dash into the shower, dry himself off and dress for the day before someone was pounding on his front door. Bumble trundled off as fast as his

little body could go. It wasn't a surprise to find Margo and Treacle waiting on the other side for them.

"Just woke up, have you?" Margo waved a cup from the local coffee shop in front of him. "Here. I brought gifts."

Grunting under his breath, George grabbed the cup. He managed a muttered "Thank you" before stumbling back into the cottage. Margo and the pups followed after him, which he'd find funny another time.

Another time when George had more brain cells awake and functioning.

He sipped the coffee and sunk down on the couch. Margo smiled when he clutched at the cup desperately.

"Why don't you two play in the garden for a minute?" Margo opened the back door, allowing Treacle and Bumble to meander outside. She eyed George with some sympathy. "Rough night?"

George gave another grunt in response.

"Right. So, a non-verbal morning. Have you eaten?"

George shook his head and took another sip of coffee.

"Okay. Well, I've got a sausage roll from the

coffee shop. It'll tide you over until we can make breakfast." Margo set the box on the table in front of him. "I'll keep an eye on the furry beasts while you remember how to human."

With a nod, George focused his energy on sipping his coffee. He was halfway through when the cobwebs cleared from his mind. The mild headache faded enough for him to not want to curse the morning.

Grabbing the box off the coffee table, George lifted the lid. He found his sausage roll, which he picked up. It was a good way to start his day off.

Or, at least, a better way.

George got to his feet and carried his coffee and roll into the garden. He stepped up beside Margo, who was watching the dogs. "Sorry."

"Always a flip of a coin whether you're going to want to converse in the mornings. I don't take it personally." Margo bent down to inspect something in the grass. She picked up a piece of paper that had been partially stuck into the ground. "This yours?"

George popped the last bite of sausage roll into his mouth to free up his hand. He grabbed the paper and inspected it. It appeared torn off from some sort of invoice. "GFL."

"What's GFL?"

"I don't know the logo. GFL." George pondered it for a second while drinking the rest of his coffee. "Griffin-Lee Logistics."

"Griffin-Lee? Belonging to Hector Griffin?"

"And someone named Lee, I presume. I've no idea. But why is it here? You'd surely have noticed if he dropped it during our argument with him." George couldn't identify anything else from the paper. He returned to the cottage and set it on the kitchen table, taking a picture and texting it to Elwin. "Sending a photo over to one of the detective constables. They're going to be cross with me."

"Not your fault. How about breakfast?"

"Pancakes?" George rifled through his cabinets. He pulled out all the ingredients. "I've got a lovely peach saffron-infused honey syrup I made last week. It'll be delightful with them."

They were sitting and eating their pancakes when Detective Constable Smith arrived. Elwin took a look at the array on the table and immediately accepted their invite to breakfast. He was the one most likely to gossip over Sarah, who was quite serious about her job.

"Did Hector Griffin have anyone with him when he came to yell about the bees?" Elwin asked between mouthfuls of pancakes.

Margo tutted at him while making a second batch. "Elwin Smith. Your gran raised you better than that."

"I'm a hungry lad." He sulked before winking at George.

"Just him and his imaginary attackers." George had been careful to avoid answering any leading questions. They'd all kept the atmosphere friendly and calm. "Why?"

"His boyfriend, Tim Frederick, insisted he saw the entire thing." Elwin held his plate up towards Margo. "Please, oh, radiant, beautiful lass, may I have another pancake?"

"You're a daft nugget." Margo smiled fondly. She plated up the last of the pancakes. "Tim Frederick. Did he move when Hector did? Name's not familiar."

"He was in the process of moving into the cottage with his boyfriend." Elwin poured a healthy amount of syrup onto his pancakes. "And you never saw him?"

"Neither time. He wasn't there when Hector Griffin confronted me by the hives or at the cottage. I'd have noticed a whole other person." George narrowed his eyes at his plate. He picked it up and moved away from the table to the sink. "Not sure I should answer these questions without my solicitor present."

"Not probing or attempting to get one over on you. I am here for the pancakes and syrup." Elwin inspected the bottle. "You make this?"

"I did. Peach, saffron, and honey from my hives." George knew Evan would likely not approve of him speaking to the detective constable, but the questions had thus far seemed innocent enough. He had no problem sticking with the truth. "Just an experiment."

"A successful one. You could bottle this." Evan dragged a slice of pancake through the excess syrup on his plate. "Do a whole range of it."

"It is bottled." George pointed to the syrup. "See? In a bottle."

"Not...." Elwin trailed off. He sent George an odd look before returning to his pancakes. "You should bottle it to sell."

It was clear to George that he'd missed something in the exchange. However, he decided there was no point in dwelling on it. He focused instead on cleaning up the dishes since Margo had been kind enough to fix pancakes for them.

Elwin finished off his pancakes in silence. He carried the plate over and handed it to George. "I'll take the paper. Not sure we can decipher much from it, but thanks for texting me."

"Have you found someone to deal with the bees?"

"DCI Baird found another local bee enthusiast who helped remove them from the property." Elwin pocketed the slip of paper. "You'll be interested to know we found no dead bees on or around Hector Griffin. We're waiting for the coroner's report on whether there's any evidence he was stung. I'll see myself out."

Waving at them, Elwin headed out of the kitchen. They heard him say goodbye to the dogs. A few seconds later, the front door opened and closed.

"Don't." Margo immediately turned to George, who'd just opened his mouth to speak. "I know what you're going to say. Don't."

"You are a ruiner of fun."

"Not a word."

"It was a video game, so technically it's a word." George finished up with the plates. He checked on Bumble to find him curled up with Treacle in a mound of blankets. "How do you see yourself out? Are you looking in a mirror when you leave?"

"I said don't." Margo sighed. She picked up the bottle of peach saffron syrup. "Have you thought about making a line of these? Elwin's not wrong. You'd sell loads."

"Seems like a lot of effort. I can make loads to give as gifts, but if you're selling, you've got many hoops to jump through. I'm pants at jumping." George enjoyed everything he did, but the idea of running a proper business overwhelmed him. "I manage fine."

"What if you had someone helping you do all the parts of a business you hate?" Margo helped him finish drying up the dishes and put them away. "How about we make a nice pot of tea and natter about it in the garden while the pups chase butterflies?"

"Sounds brilliant." George had just reached for the kettle when someone rang the doorbell. "Oh for—"

Assuming Elwin had returned for another question, George went to open the door. He carefully dodged Treacle and Bumble, who'd been woken up by the sound. They followed him closely.

"What is it now?" George yanked open the door and frowned. "You're not Elwin."

"Who?" A woman with coppery red hair and brown eyes frowned at him. She stood beside a taller man with a strong jaw and piercing blue eyes. "I'm Felicity Griffin. This is Marcello Lee."

Lee and Griffin.

Griffin-Lee.

George immediately regretted opening the door. He had no interest in being yelled at or accused of anything. "Did you need something?"

"May we come in?"

"Why?" George sighed when Margo stepped up beside him and eased in front of him.

"Hello. I'm Margo Sheth, and this is my cousin George. It's his cottage. Ignore the furry beasts at our feet. The most they'll do is lick you to death." She took charge of the situation, which was brilliant because he didn't enjoy dealing with strangers. "We were about to have a spot of tea in the garden. Would you like to join us?"

"Thank you." Felicity nodded. She seemed a little confused but readily followed Margo through the cottage.

George fidgeted awkwardly while Marcello Lee stood in front of him. "Going to join them?"

"Hector Griffin was my business partner—and her brother. We came by to tell you that despite what Hector's little toyboy claims, we don't believe you murdered him. He moved in barely a week ago, if that." Marcello continued on without noticing how tense George had become. "As annoying as he could be, I highly doubt he managed to piss off a complete stranger badly enough to kill him."

"I... thank you?" George wasn't quite sure what the appropriate response should be. He cursed Margo for abandoning him. "Thank you."

Attempting a welcoming smile, George stepped back into the cottage. He dodged Bumble and Treacle, tripping over the latter. Marcello lunged forward to catch him and keep him from falling.

"Careful. It wouldn't do for you to bash your head against the wall." Marcello's smile felt off to George, but he couldn't figure out why. "Everything all right?"

"Fine. Brilliant. Thanks." George tried not to scowl when it took a moment longer for Marcello to let go of his arms. "Garden's through there. Follow the dogs."

There was another moment of uneasy silence until Marcello nodded. George turned back towards the front door; the man could find his way outside. He gave a full-body shudder, trying to shake off the uncomfortable feeling.

Why had they come over to his cottage? What

was the point? He didn't think either of the detectives would've suggested it.

It all had a slightly unsavoury vibe. George wanted to kick them out of his home. He knew it wouldn't be polite, but he wasn't sure he cared.

Margo would care. She did small talk and politeness better than he ever could. He just couldn't bring himself to stress over the artifice of neurotypical niceties.

Spotting his vlogging camera on the side, George went over to turn it on. He didn't trust them at all. Either of them. Their smiles felt like they'd stretched their mouths too far, like a canvas pulled too tightly over a frame.

"And what do you do?" Marcello feigned interest well, but George didn't buy it. "With your bees?"

"What do I do with them?" George raised his eyebrows at the man. He parsed the words in his mind, trying to figure out the right answer. "I sell the honey to a local brewery for their mead."

"Ah. How interesting." Marcello didn't sound all that intrigued. He smothered a yawn before offering another one of those smiles. "And you can afford all of this by selling honey?"

"I can." George leaned forward in the chair to

pet Bumble, who'd bumped into his leg. "It's all right, bumblebee. I'm good."

The small talk continued for several minutes. George slowly devolved into yes or no answers. He had no idea what the two were attempting to do. Why had they come over to say hello?

Were they really just trying to be friendly?

They didn't seem to be the type.

"Mind if I use your loo?" Felicity finally brought an end to the painful attempts at friendly conversation. "I imagine we'll be on our way then."

Thank god.

George wanted to say no. He hated strangers being in his space, but Margo sent him a pointed look. "Inside, just off the kitchen to the left."

She would not need to go down the hall to his bedroom and the en suite. Instead, she could use the water closet. George couldn't wait to have his cottage to himself; he knew he was getting increasingly overwhelmed.

He desperately needed time to decompress. A few hours spent with one of his favourite shows that he'd seen a million times would help, as would just the quiet emptiness of having no one but Bumble and bees around. He hoped Margo wouldn't take it personally when he kicked her out.

After what felt like hours, a smiling Felicity joined them in the garden once again. She seemed anxious to leave after spending so much time dithering. Marcello followed her lead; they said their goodbyes and were gone before George could do more than wave.

George glanced over at Margo. They were both still standing in the garden when they heard the front door slam shut. "That was odd, right? Not just me... being me."

"Very, very odd."

"My camera." George suddenly remembered he'd left it on inside the cottage. He darted inside with a confused Margo following behind. "I thought maybe they might try something, so I wanted proof."

"And? Did you catch something?"

"No idea." George grabbed his laptop off his desk and returned to the living room. He hooked the camera up to the computer, cursing when he got the USB in wrong the first four times. "Oh for...."

"Here." Margo gently took the cord from him and got it in on the first try.

"Witchcraft," George teased. "That is not normal. Any other tricks to share?"

"My only talent."

"This might take a minute to upload." George

genuinely didn't think he had a lot of conversation left in him.

"Why don't I take Treacle home? You can pop by later or tomorrow to show me the video." Margo hugged him before calling for her dog. "Try not to get yourself in any more trouble."

"Not funny."

EIGHT

MURPHY

"How? How is it even possible in the space of a month, you and your boyfriend are accused of murder?" Teagan had lined up the ingredients for one of their early autumn batches of mead. They'd get everything prepped now to make the rest of the process easier. "Honestly. It has to be some sort of bizarre record. Can we call the Guinness Book of World Records? Who's next? Me? Bumble?"

"Tea." Murphy massaged his forehead. He hadn't gotten enough sleep with worrying about George. "Not right now, please?"

"You all right, Paddy?" Teagan set aside the herbs and walked around their work table. They wrapped an arm around his shoulder. "He'll be okay. No one could possibly believe George murdered

someone, especially if it meant potential harm to his bees."

"True. Stranger things have happened."

"What? Like two people dropping dead near you?" Teagan dodged away from him when he growled at them. "Have you seen the decorations in the pub?"

Murphy rolled his eyes at the sudden change of subject but allowed it so he could stop thinking about George being arrested. "I have. Feels like I've been transported into ancient times."

"Maisie's brilliant. I still say we should've done this for a Halloween theme instead of in the middle of summer." Teagan made an excellent point.

"I said the same thing."

"And?"

"Maisie is a force unto herself. I'm not going to try to change her mind. Graeme's the one who married her. She's not my problem." Murphy did think his sister-in-law had done a fantastic job with the decorations. It was a tad moody for the middle of summer. "Well, if nothing else, it'll be a change of pace."

"True enough. And I suppose Maisie has a point. The blackberry and caramelised honey is darker than our usual summer flavours. The druid theme works." Teagan grabbed their recipe journal. They'd already created a page for the new experiment. "Did you make your plans for your date tonight?"

"We're having a date night in."

"*Paddington.*"

"George had a rough night. A tough few days. He's already overwhelmed by circumstances, so he asked if we could get a takeaway. Who am I to say no?" Murphy didn't mind staying at the cottage. He'd prefer not to deal with half the village "popping" in to say hello and spy on their date. *Gossipy bastards.* "We'll watch a movie and enjoy ourselves."

"Fine, fine." Teagan raised their hands in surrender. "Who am I to attempt to bring something new into your lives?"

"New is stressful for George," Murphy pointed out. "It takes him a while to work himself up to doing it. Not sure this is the week for it."

"It doesn't hurt that you'd rather boil your own arm than deal with people most days."

"Boil my own arm?" Murphy eyed them warily for a second before they dissolved into laughter. "What've you been watching on the telly?"

"Margo and I did a horror movie marathon."

"Margo and I?" Murphy mimicked their tone, smirking when they scowled at him. "Not sure I want to know what happened in those movies if boiling my arm was the first idea you latched onto."

With all of their ingredients pulled together, Murphy put all his attention on brewing up a batch of mead. They were continuing their experiment with caramelised honey. Teagan had come up with an idea for an apple-cinnamon mead.

They hoped, with the addition of the honey, it would come out tasting almost like a salted-caramel, apple-cinnamon mead. Murphy supposed it might more appropriately be considered a cider. They hadn't played with it; he hoped to create a full autumnal-flavoured line from their first experimentation.

"Yeast is all hydrated and ready." Teagan hefted up the container they'd used. It had a bit of apple juice along with the aforementioned yeast to get the process started. "Is the honey warm enough to start?"

"Yeah, go on. Let's get to mixing."

As per usual, Murphy found everything else faded away. He lost himself in the process of making mead. They'd been at it for a couple of hours before the alarm Teagan set on their phone went off.

They had an amazing knack for getting the timing just right. Murphy had sealed up the last container. He carried them back into the storeroom, finding an open space on one of the many shelves. Teagan followed behind him and put labels on all of them.

It was late in the afternoon when Murphy finally left the brewery. George had initially texted to cancel their date. But an hour or so later, he'd changed his mind.

After picking up a takeaway from the local fish and chip shop, Murphy drove through the village to the cottage. George was definitely not himself when he opened the door. His long hair was all over the place like he'd pulled it out of the tie in parts, leaving it hanging by a thread.

Or a hair.

"George?" Murphy set the bag of food on the kitchen counter and returned to where a muttering George remained by the door. "What's happened?"

"Someone's trying to frame me for murder."

Murphy caught George's hands to stop him from tugging on his hair. "Okay. Okay. Easy. Let's take this one step at a time."

Using his hold on George's hands, Murphy led him into the living room. He spotted a brush on a bookshelf, so he grabbed it. A concerned Bumble watched from his bed on the floor.

First, pulling out the tie, Murphy gently ran his

fingers through George's long black hair. He carefully removed the worst of the tangles before doing anything else. A few runs through with the brush helped smooth out the rest.

After about ten minutes, Murphy managed to get George's hair back into its usual sleek ponytail. He set the brush to the side. It was good to see his boyfriend beginning to relax.

His shoulders had lowered, and his fists unclenched at his side. He'd also stopped muttering about being framed. Murphy finally released him and moved off the couch to give him space.

Murphy went into the kitchen and began pulling packets out of the takeaway bag. "If you didn't want anyone around, I wouldn't have minded taking a rain check."

"I don't mind you. People insist on talking or asking what's wrong. You're content to sit and enjoy being together without speaking." George lapsed into silence again. He eventually moved off the couch to join Murphy. "You don't demand things from me when I'm overwhelmed."

Settling into a companionable quiet, they plated up their dinners. George doused his chips and fish with a sweet chilli sauce. Another of his own recipes. They took their food and drinks, going out into the garden to enjoy the light summer breeze that had come after a brief storm.

"They're trying to frame me."

"Who?" Murphy swallowed the handful of chips he'd shoved into his mouth. "Why?"

"Felicity Griffin."

"Felicity Griffin? Related to Hector?"

"The sister. She came over with her brother's business partner. Marcello. He smiled oddly at me. Very disconcerting. I didn't like it or him." George dragged a chunk of fish through some of the chilli sauce. "She went into the cottage while we were outside. I left my camera on. She was definitely snooping around."

"What makes you think she was trying to frame you?" Murphy balanced his plate on his knee, focusing his attention on George. "Did you catch her doing something dodgy on camera?"

"Maybe?" George wiped his fingers clean and got to his feet. "You want to see the video?"

"Of course." Murphy popped the last bite of fish into his mouth and stood up as well. "Dinner with a little light entertainment? The perfect date."

"I'm not sure this qualifies as entertainment." George grabbed Murphy's plate and popped both into the sink. "We can watch on my laptop. It's on the sofa."

The video wasn't all that long. Murphy leaned into George with the laptop perched on their knees, bending forward to get a better look. The woman on the screen appeared to snoop all around the cottage, in view of the camera, before disappearing into the loo.

In all, it was maybe ten minutes. A long time for someone who just needed to go to the toilet. But not suspicious in and of itself, Murphy did find it odd.

"What makes you think she's trying to frame you?" Murphy hadn't seen anything overly incriminating on the video. "She's definitely nosy, but that's not criminal behaviour."

"Invasive, maybe. I agree. It made me uncomfortable, but anyone in my space does that aside from a handful of people." George set the laptop on the coffee table. "I found something—and I don't know what to do with it."

"Okay." Murphy was suddenly more concerned than he'd been earlier. "What did you find?"

George stood up and motioned for Murphy to follow him. He led him to the tiny loo off the kitchen, stepping inside and opening the medicine cabinet. "See?"

"What am I looking at?"

George gestured to a small tub of eye cream. "I've never seen this before in my life. I don't use any sort of cosmetics or other skincare. I haven't touched it because I don't want my fingerprints on it."

"Wise move."

"What do I do?" George waved wildly around the small space. "I mean, she's obviously trying to frame me, right? Why else is this here?"

"Could anyone other than Felicity Griffin have placed it here?" Murphy knew it was a question the detectives would ask. "Anyone at all."

"Margo didn't. I asked. It's not mine. Aside from Felicity. Maybe a random ghost? Marcello Lee could've done it while my back was turned, but... I don't know." George stepped closer to Murphy, who eased him into a hug.

Murphy ran his hand up and down George's back. "Okay. We're going to call Evan first and have a chat with him. I imagine he'll want to be here before the police."

"Sarah's going to be angry."

"She'll be mildly annoyed, but this isn't your fault."

"Do we have to call her?" George dropped his head against Murphy's chest and grumbled creative curses under his breath for a few seconds. "They might not find out."

"George."

"I'm being ridiculous. I just need a moment to whinge about it. I'm aware this was placed for the purpose of being found." George eased back from Murphy. He pushed him in the chest until he backed out of the loo. "You call Evan. He's going to yell."

"He'll...." Murphy trailed off. He considered the number of hours George had been in possession of the video and the potentially tainted pot of cream. "He might shout a little."

NINE

GEORGE

ONCE EVAN GOT THE SHOUTING OUT OF HIS system, he mildly suggested they touch nothing. He told them to leave the loo and wait for him. They could contact the police together once he'd arrived.

"Touch. Nothing."

George could hear Evan's voice clear across the room from where Murphy was on the phone with him. "He sounded angry."

Murphy shoved his phone into his back pocket. "He'll be fine. What else did he intend for his life when he decided to become a solicitor?"

"Not being interrupted in the middle of the night for potentially venom-laced skincare?" George perched on the arm of the sofa.

Murphy wondered while tapping away at his

phone. "Sent a text to him with the photos. He can shout at me for a second time via message. If the venom is in the skincare, how much would you need to put into it to cause an allergic reaction? A little? A lot? Would someone even notice it?"

"Probably depends on the level of the allergy. One sting can send someone into anaphylactic shock, so how much venom does one bee hold?" George grabbed his phone, intending to do a quick Google search but set it back down a second later. "Maybe it's not something I should have readily available in my internet history."

"Probably not." Murphy was serious for half a second before they both grinned. "Can you imagine Sarah's face?"

"I'd rather not. She's going to hate me. Or arrest me." George groaned. He gave a slightly hysterical chuckle. "Is it possible we have the worst luck possible with people dropping dead not long after arguing with us?"

"Coincidence." Murphy waved off his concern.

"Twice in the space of a month?"

"An odd and creepy coincidence but still not necessarily a conspiracy." Murphy slipped off the arm of the couch and came over to draw him into a hug. "It's going to be okay."

"If this happens a third time, I'm going to start thinking we've been cursed by a druid or something." George glanced down when Bumble bumped into his ankle. "Were you being ignored?"

Bending down to pick him up, George cuddled Bumble between their bodies. It didn't take long for the pug to start wiggling around. He set him back on the floor and moved away from Murphy when his phone buzzed.

"Evan?"

"Yelling at me in all caps not to do or touch anything until he's here. Think we might have to give him a bonus." Murphy slipped his phone back into his pocket. "He'll be here as soon as possible. We can wait to call Sarah or Elwin. The little pot isn't going anywhere."

"I might be."

"Think positively."

"I definitely will be." George loosened the tie on his hair and redid the ponytail. He needed to do something with his hands to keep them from trembling. His anxiety had shot up again after finally feeling relaxed. "I definitely will be positively unsurprised if I am brought in for questioning with a potential murder weapon found in my sodding loo."

"Please don't use sodding and loo in the same sentence." Murphy grimaced. He was obviously trying to lighten the mood since George had started to spiral into dark and panicky thoughts. "Sarah will listen. Evan believes us, and he'll force them to listen."

"It's not like last month when you were accused. I don't have cameras or witnesses who saw me across the room. The only thing in my favour is I don't really have a motive." George slumped into the couch. He tossed his phone onto the cushion beside him. "Aside from him coming over to yell about the bees."

"If she did murder him, why would she choose to frame you?"

"Convenience? She heard him complaining about my bees and decided it made a perfect foil for her murderous plot." George draped his arm over his face and pretended for a moment their summer hadn't turned into a bizarre true crime series. "They aren't from around here. They don't know me. If this is part of a plan, I'd wager I'm a last-minute addition."

"A frame opportunity?"

With a shrug, George fell silent for a few minutes. He hoped the detectives were willing to keep an open mind. It definitely looked highly suspicious.

"I'll make up a pot of coffee for us. We're going to need the fortification." Murphy disappeared into the kitchen. "Biscuits as well."

The brief respite from chaos helped George settle his nerves. Evan arrived when they were several biscuits and half a cup of coffee into their fortification. He immediately insisted on seeing the video footage before they tried explaining.

"Right. Tell me about this little pot you found." Evan watched the video three times before he spoke. "Where was it, and did you touch it?"

"I'll show you." George led him to the loo. He pointed out the little cabinet. They'd left the door open so he could see it easily. "She spent so much time in here that it made me suspicious. After they left, I decided to check if she'd mucked about. I've never seen the eye cream. I've never used a product like it. And neither of us has touched it. I didn't want my fingerprints on it."

"Well, that's something, at least." Evan leaned in closer to get a better look at the pot. "There's an import sticker on this—Griffin-Lee Logistics. Another point in your favour. Hopefully, the police will be able to track it down. Okay. We're giving

Detective Constable Smith a call since I doubt he'll be quite as annoyed as your cousin."

"You are correct." Murphy scratched at his beard absently, glancing over at George, who could only shrug. "Elwin's going to call Sarah, so I imagine we'll hear her opinion whether we told her directly or not."

"Better to head things off." Evan pursed his lips, still staring at the pot in the cabinet. "And you're certain you've never touched it."

"Never. Not when I found out. I opened the cabinet and spotted it." George had kept far away once he'd seen it. "I don't even think I breathed on it, in all honesty."

"Excellent. You'll want to make sure to have a ready copy of the video you took. Have you messaged Margo? They will likely want to chat with her since she was here when they visited." Evan checked his phone when it buzzed in his hand. "All right. I've had one of the other solicitors at the firm pulling what's readily available information there was on Griffin-Lee Logistics."

"Anything interesting?"

"Two things jump out at me immediately. First, Felicity Griffin was a joint share-holder in the company before she was forced out. There are a few business articles about it. And, second, a quite public disagreement between the remaining partners about whether to move their warehouse." Evan was silent for a second while he continued to read the messages coming into his phone. "Also, my mate heard from his sister that Hector Griffin had just broken up with his boyfriend."

"The one who told the detectives about Hector's argument with me? The one who basically fingered me for the murder?" George needed a moment to process everything Evan had just told them. "I need coffee."

Despite the lateness of the hour, George went to get a second cup of coffee. After that, he wanted nothing more than to crawl into bed with his head-phones and a blanket over his head. But since that wasn't going to happen, he'd settle for another drink and a handful of biscuits.

"Can I help you?" George glanced down at Bumble, who followed him into the kitchen and flopped down with his head on George's foot. He refused to budge. "Are you wanting a treat? Is this a hint? It's past your bedtime."

Sacrificing a tiny piece of cheese to Bumble freed George's foot. He returned his attention to filling the coffee pot and getting it going. It felt like the day was never going to end.

George leaned forward with his hands gripping the counter and tried to stretch out his back, anything to relieve the tension flooding through him. Bumble appeared between his legs, peering up at him. "It's all going to be okay."

Bumble sadly had no grand words of wisdom for him. George gave him a tiny treat and then hunted one of his own. He spotted a little container of biscuits Margo had brought over for him, another of her experiments with shortbread.

These had cashews and a few spices. He nibbled on one while waiting for the coffee to finish. Murphy joined him midway through his biscuit.

"Elwin and Sarah are on the way. Surprisingly no shouting. They did make us promise not to touch anything in the loo." Murphy rubbed his hand over George's back. "It's going to be okay. Evan won't let them arrest you."

"Not sure Evan has that sort of power." George tried to think positively. They'd surely believe him when they saw the video and checked the pot for fingerprints. "Why would someone do this to me?"

"Framing someone is probably nothing at all if they're willing to kill a person." Murphy snagged one of the biscuits and tossed it into his mouth. "Just listen to Evan."

"Evan's going to stop answering our calls at this point."

"Not if he wants to get paid." Murphy smiled when they heard Evan tell him off from the room. "What? You're not doing charity work."

"Why am I friends with you?" Evan posed his rhetorical question while reaching between them to grab one of the shortbread biscuits for himself. "Is there a coffee for me? I need my brain functioning on all cylinders."

"All good things come to those who wait." George grabbed an extra mug for Evan. "Should I make some for the detectives?"

"Might make them less narky." Murphy considered his words for a second. "It is late at night, and we've found a potential murder weapon in the loo. So, on second thought, nothing is going to make Sarah less narky."

"I feel loads better. Thanks."

"Now, who's being narky?" Murphy grinned when George swatted him on the arm. "It's going to be okay."

"I hope so."

TEN

MURPHY

The detectives arrived together. Elwin took the lead, which didn't surprise Murphy. Sarah stood behind him, glowering at all of them. She hadn't said anything yet; he knew she was holding on for the beautiful rant that would come at some point.

Murphy was almost disappointed when they simply took George's statement, a copy of the video, and collected the evidence. He exchanged a confused look with the others when they'd left. "Was it anticlimactic for anyone else?"

"No yelling." George sank down on the couch. He covered his face with a cushion for a moment, mumbling muffled curses into it. "Why do I feel more concerned?"

"Don't allow anyone connected to Griffin into

your cottage. And if the detectives come 'round again, give me a call." Evan chugged down the last of his coffee before heading towards the door. "Try to keep it during normal business hours if at all possible."

"Yes, we'll definitely schedule any and all legal issues to a nine-to-five window." Murphy smirked when Evan flipped him off. "Tell Teagan hello."

"Wanker." Evan slammed the door shut behind him.

Murphy shook his head at the dramatics. He turned to find George with his head in his hands. "The detectives know you didn't kill him. We don't even know what's in the eye cream. No point in stressing at the moment."

"And yet, here I am. Still stressed." George collapsed against the cushions with a groan. "You realise my dad and yours are descending into the middle of this madness."

"Bugger. I'd forgotten." Murphy dropped onto the sofa beside George. He threw his arm around him and drew him into his side. "Sarah's not going to be thrilled when they begin sticking their noses into her inquiry."

"They wouldn't."

"Your dad would move heaven and earth for you.

And I'm fairly confident mine loves you more than me," Murphy teased. "Can you imagine either of them deciding to ignore a murder inquiry?"

"Well, no. But only because they're cut from the same interfering cloth." George had an excellent point.

Duncan Baird and Rishi Sheth had become the best of mates several years ago during the Highland Games when they'd both been visiting their respective sons and met each other. It had been like long-lost brothers reconnecting. The two were inseparable.

"They're going to want to know about us." Murphy had deflected questions about their relationship. Neither of them wanted to be overloaded with questions from their families when they'd only just started dating—officially. "And they're definitely going to be obnoxious about shoving themselves into the investigation."

George yawned in response. "They're going to be who they are. I say we let Detectives Smith and Baird deal with the issues of parental interference."

Murphy had to chuckle at the visual of Sarah attempting to corral the two older men into behaving themselves. "Brilliant. Right. If you keep yawning like that, you'll crack your jaw. Think it's time for bed."

"Stay?" George picked absently at a thread on the cushion in his lap. "To sleep?"

Murphy squeezed his arm around George a little more tightly. "Of course."

In no time at all, George was fast asleep, cuddled beside Murphy. Bumble was snoring somewhere close to their feet. It took him far longer to drift off.

Murphy tightened his hold. It wasn't the first time they'd slept together like this. He took great pleasure in knowing George was so comfortable in his presence. *We're going to figure this out.*

Sarah and Elwin's departure concerned him. Murphy found it odd they hadn't wanted to ask more questions. He hadn't wanted George to see how much it worried him.

Were they waiting to bring George in for more official questioning?

It was an hour or more before Murphy managed to fall asleep. He woke up to George with his head on his shoulder and a snuffling Bumble on his chest. It brought a contented smile to his face.

Bumble inched up his chest and bumped into his chin. Murphy generally woke up in something of a bad mood. He didn't often find himself wanting to smile so early in the morning.

"Are you wanting a walk?" Murphy tilted his head to peer down at the pug, who butted into his chin for a second time. He chuckled when Bumble rubbed his head against his beard. "Are you cleaning your eyes out on my face?"

"It could be worse." George groggily sat up in bed. He stretched his arms over his head before finally reaching out to lift Bumble into his arms. "Come on. Up you get."

"Me or Bumble?"

"Both. Or did you forget the parental invasion on the way? I wouldn't put it past them to arrive early just because they can't wait to meet up and get here." George did have an excellent point. It wouldn't be the first time one of Murphy's family members had caught him off guard on purpose. "Besides, the garden and bees won't take care of themselves. Fancy breakfast? I can throw together a quick omelette. Still have some of the bread Margo baked."

"Why don't you let our little bumblebee out into the garden? I'll splash some water on my face and get coffee going." Murphy sat up in bed as well. He needed to call his brother and see how preparations at the pub were coming. "I'll give Graeme and Maisie a shout. They can provide a distraction."

"They're a distraction most days without having to try." George waved Bumble's paw at him before heading out the door.

Murphy collapsed back on the bed with a groan. They'd spent the night cuddled together in bed. His mind was drifting off into thoughts of George when he heard the doorbell. "Shite."

Scrambling out of bed, Murphy shoved his feet into his trainers and tried to quickly make his way to the front door. He hoped to save George from dealing with any annoyances so early in the morning. He'd half-expected to find their dads, but instead, it was a complete stranger.

"Yes?" Murphy didn't know what to make of the younger man in front of him. He seemed sad and almost sheepish. "Have we met?"

"I... no. I don't think so. I'm Tim Frederick."

The name didn't mean anything to Murphy, so he simply nodded in acknowledgement. They stood in increasingly uncomfortable silence for several seconds. Tim opened his mouth several times but couldn't seem to put his thoughts together.

"Was there something you needed?" Murphy eventually prompted when the silence continued.

"I've come to apologise. I think a misspoken comment of mine might've grown legs and walked away." Tim dragged his fingers through already messy brown hair. "Hector and I were in a relationship."

"Ah."

"We were in love," Tim insisted almost defensively. "I was distraught when we found him. I... mentioned the argument he'd had with your friend. But I never insinuated he was involved in Hector's death. Not once."

"Oh?" Murphy recalled the detectives mentioning a friend of the victim had pointed them in George's direction. "Did you not?"

"No. I only said he'd recently confronted someone. He had a temper. I often had to talk him out of a sulk or tantrum. But Felicity was the one to suggest the police look into your friend. Honest." Tim sniffled. He dragged the sleeve of his shirt across his eyes. "I'm terribly sorry about all of this. Is your friend okay? Was his name Gerry?"

"George. His name is George. I'm Murphy, by the way. I own the mead brewery and pub down the lane." He didn't want to invite the man into the cottage, but it felt callous to leave him crying on the stoop. "Do you have family here? Or someone who can offer you support?"

"Felicity and Marcello are handling everything. I'm just...." Tim dropped his hands to his side and gave a half-hearted shrug. "Adrift."

"Invite him in," George muttered from behind him, startling Murphy, who hadn't heard him approach. "I've got a pot of tea brewing and some bread in the toaster."

With a resigned sigh, Murphy stepped back and waved the teary-eyed Tim into the cottage. He had no doubts Evan would get quite vocally annoyed with them. But it was hard not to be moved by the obviously genuine emotion of the man.

"Are you sure?"

"Go on. He's got tea and toast." Murphy motioned for Tim to head down the hall. He closed the door and stared at it for a few moments. *And this is why I hate dealing with people in the morning. It's too sodding early for tears.*

ELEVEN

GEORGE

THEY'D BEEN WARNED TO AVOID HAVING ANYONE connected to Hector Griffin in the cottage. But George hadn't been able to ignore the grieving boyfriend. He also believed what the man had said.

It was entirely plausible that George's name had come into the conversation in shock and grief. He'd gone through a few pieces of toast while Tim pulled himself together. Bumble provided much-needed comic relief by zooming around the kitchen like a bee had stung him.

"Calm down, bumblebee." George gave him the tiny sliver of bread crust. "Why don't we head into the garden?"

Over the course of breakfast, Tim had painted

the picture of a perfect relationship with Hector. He seemed to be genuinely grieving for his boyfriend. But oddly, he'd bolted the second Evan had called Murphy.

"What did you think of him?" Murphy strolled into the garden, still clutching his third mug of tea. "Tim?"

"Seemed sad." George shrugged. "A bit strange how he was in a hurry to leave when we mentioned our solicitor coming over."

"More than a bit odd." Murphy took another sip of his tea. "We should tell Evan about Tim coming to see us."

"Not it." George immediately raised his hands and backed away.

"But he likes you better."

"Does not." George whistled for Bumble, who stopped trying to catch a butterfly. "I can safely say he's equally irritated with the both of us. And I'm a terrible judge of someone's emotions, so that should tell you how frustrated he is."

"I don't know why. We're giving him plenty of business." Murphy shifted his mug into his other hand, stepped closer, and wrapped his arm around George's shoulders. "It was nice waking up to you cuddling against my chest this morning."

George hid his embarrassed grin against his own mug of tea. "It was. Nice."

Nice didn't seem to be the right word for it. George slid his arm around Murphy's back. They stood together, watching Bumble continue to chase his butterfly.

Their oasis of calm was disrupted by Evan's arrival. George veered off into the kitchen while letting Murphy answer the door. Again. It was almost like they lived together—a dream for another day.

"Pardon? I can't have heard you right." Evan strode into the kitchen with Murphy behind him. "You once again invited someone connected to the murdered victim into your home? For a chat? What did I tell you? Have you both absolutely lost the plot? All of it. Entirely. Lost it. You're being accused of killing him. Why are you sitting down to tea with them?"

"No, but I think you might have. Sit down. We'll make some tea."

"Tea? Do you want him to be arrested for murder?" Evan glowered at Murphy before slumping into one of the kitchen chairs. "Fine. Tea. And biscuits. I need sugar."

"You need something, but I'm not sure it's

sugar." Murphy came to give George a hand putting tea together yet again. "You didn't see him."

"And you shouldn't have either," Evan grumbled.

"Fair enough. Berate us after you've heard the story." Murphy dropped his hands on George's shoulders, lightly massaging them. He bent his head forward. "He'll calm down."

"He can hear you." Evan grabbed the container of shortbread Murphy held out to him. "Okay. I shall calm myself and listen."

While Murphy gave him a brief recap of the conversation, George cleaned the kitchen up from breakfast. He finally settled into one of the seats with a fresh mug of tea. It wasn't a surprise to find that Evan had finished the last shortbread biscuit.

"Detective Constable Smith called me with an update." Evan brushed his fingers clean and pushed the biscuit container away. "You were apparently correct about the bees found in the Griffin cottage. They found no signs of the deceased being stung. They're testing the cream found in your cabinet. They found a fingerprint on the container, so I imagine they'll be comparing it to yours and anyone else on their suspect list."

"I'm probably their entire suspect list." George

knew he was being ever so slightly fatalistic in his thoughts. He held a hand up to stop Evan and Murphy from trying to reassure him. "I'm aware that was hyperbolic. But it's how everything feels at the moment."

"We're not going to allow anyone to lock you up for something you didn't do," Murphy promised.

"Not sure it's always as simple as that." George had read enough to know innocent until proven guilty didn't necessarily mean justice got it right the first time. "We'll figure it out."

Their conversation was cut short by yet another knock on the door. George wondered if he should just take to sitting in the front garden at this point. He'd never had so many visitors in one morning before.

"I'll get it." Murphy disappeared down the hall. They heard the door open and then a boisterous hello. "Incoming."

George bent forward to lightly bang his head on the table. "Shite."

"What?"

"The parental invasion is early." George got to his feet. He had no doubts that he was about to be squeezed to death by both men. Being overly affectionate was something the two fathers had in common. "You can always make a run for it."

"You're being dramatic." Evan grinned at him. "Besides, I've met Rishi and Duncan before. It's always entertaining to watch Paddy be treated like he's a small child."

"For you. Maybe not so much for him or me." George had just made his way around the kitchen table when he heard his father calling out beta, or son. "Abba."

"Ah. My son. My only son." His father stomped over to him, grabbing him by the shoulders and holding him at a distance. He kissed him on both cheeks and then dragged him into a tight hug. "Ah, beta. How have you been? Are you eating enough? What's this I hear about a murder investigation? Another one?"

The questions continued to pour out of his dad while George simply stood there being hugged to death. He was finally released after what felt like hours. Unfortunately, Murphy was being treated similarly by his own father.

Duncan Baird bore a striking resemblance to his eldest son. His personality was all Graeme, however. Boisterous and cheery, the patriarch of the Baird clan was a slightly rounder and significantly greyer version of Murphy.

"Well? Answer my questions." Rishi made his way into the kitchen, acknowledging Evan with a nod before going to inspect the contents of his refrigerator. "Why am I only hearing about this murder from your uncle? Hmm?"

"Abba." George pinched the bridge of his nose and prayed for patience from any deity he could think of. "It happened two days ago. There wasn't anything to tell you. It's fine."

"Fine?" He frowned before returning to hunting through the various containers. "Fine? How is this fine? Have you been eating enough? Your mother worries."

"Abba." George tried for a second time. He massaged his forehead while trying not to laugh. "Abba. I eat. I'm fine. I can cook. You taught me, remember? I can cook. I can clean. I can do all of the things."

"Of course, you can. You're my son, and you're brilliant, but are you eating enough?" He pulled out a container of leftovers Margo had brought over for him. "I sense the hand of your cousin."

"I'm happy to see you too, Abba." George grabbed the kettle and refilled it. "Tea?"

"With a splash of something stronger?"

"Would Mum approve?" George nodded towards the cabinet, where he had a few bottles of alcohol. "Take your pick."

"Mum is on a trip. She doesn't have to know." He winked at his son. "Now, now, what's this I hear about you and Paddington Bear?"

"Oh shite," George muttered. He felt like his mind was spinning from the multiple changes in subjects. "We're...."

"We stopped by the brewery first. Graeme mentioned he hadn't seen you this morning." Duncan threw his arm around his son. His smile was as wide as Rishi's when he turned to glance at George. "Now, are you treating my wee bairn well?"

"Wee bairn?" Evan choked on a laugh. "Murphy? A wee bairn? What a glorious day. I might not even charge you for my time."

"Well? Is he treating you well?" Duncan turned his attention to his son. "And you? Are you behaving yourself? I hope not."

While their dads roared with laughter, Murphy sent George a commiserating and sympathetic smile. There was no stopping Rishi and Duncan when they were together. They could be genuinely exhausting when they so desired.

"And you." Duncan swung around to face Evan, who froze while taking a sip of his tea. "Why haven't you dealt with the police?"

"I...." Evan didn't seem to know what to do when faced with the attention of both fathers. "I'm working on it—and they keep inviting people connected to the victim into the cottage."

George groaned when two parental tornadoes twisted in his direction. "I was taught to be polite. Was I supposed to slam the door in their faces?"

"Yes," they chorused together.

"Right. Sure. I'll remember that for next time." George was thankful when the kettle went off. He needed the distraction and the caffeine boost, even if he'd probably had too many cups for one morning. "And I didn't exactly send an invitation for them to come over. They showed up all on their own without my help."

While Duncan and Rishi began to ramble about suspicious behaviour, George prepped the mugs for tea. He let it brew for several minutes. The conversation still flowed without his input, thankfully. It gave him time to settle a little.

He'd had such hopes for the day.

Such hopes.

Waking up with Murphy's arms wrapped

around him had been perfection. It had been everything he'd ever hoped it would be. And he'd certainly had more dreams than he'd ever want to admit to having.

George was just pouring the tea when his doorbell rang for what felt like the hundredth time. "Did I invite the entire sodding village?"

"I'll answer."

George immediately cringed when his father dodged everyone else to head for the door. "Abba."

His father ignored him. George followed after him, wanting to make sure they didn't have an incident. He blanched when the door swung open to reveal Detective Constable Smith and Constable Natalie Bettley. She was a lovely woman whose girlfriend was part of his online bee enthusiast community.

"George? We'd like you to come have a chat with us." Elwin's smile seemed oddly uncomfortable to him. "I'm guessing your solicitor is here? I spotted Chan's car. Why don't you grab him and meet us at the station in Keith? There are a few questions we have for you."

George's gaze darted from one person to the other. He finally settled on Murphy, trying to sound calm and collected when he wanted to scream into a pillow for an hour. "I haven't even checked on the bees yet."

TWELVE

MURPHY

The cottage had been unbearable with just their fathers and Bumble. Murphy had left them alone after Margo texted to say she'd go over to ensure they didn't set the place on fire. One never knew what Rishi Sheth and Duncan Baird might get themselves into.

He was less concerned about fire and more about them deciding to confront Hector Griffin's friends and family. They'd been concerned once George had left with the police and his solicitor. But he couldn't sit around and wait for news.

Murphy had gone first to the brewery to check on everyone there. He slammed things around in his office, trying to distract himself until someone tapped on his open door. "What?"

"If you don't calm yourself, you're going to break something or give yourself a heart attack." Teagan was ever the voice of reason. They leaned against the doorframe, far more relaxed than Murphy could manage. "Evan's with him. He won't let them talk circles around George. Why didn't you head to Keith if you were so wound up?"

"I didn't trust myself not to storm the station and demand to be in the interrogation room. I'm not trying to cause trouble for the detectives." Murphy collapsed into his office chair. He scratched absently at his beard while trying to reel his temper back in. "If I tried to work on mead right now, I'd make the bitterest brew in history."

"Why don't we try to help George?"

"How?" Murphy tilted his chair back, rocking a little in it. "What can we do to prove he's innocent?"

"Nothing, but we can prove someone else is guilty."

"Isn't it the same thing?" Murphy raised an eyebrow in confusion. "Sounds quite similar."

"Not exactly. Listen, we know the three people mostly likely to have been involved. Why don't we see what we can do to bring the real killer to light? If nothing else, it'll keep you from stomping around like a bear with a thorn in its paw." Teagan tapped their knuckles against the doorframe lightly. "Well? Might as well see if we can find them. Evan'll give you a call if anything changes."

"I should be there."

"And make a nuisance of yourself or get yourself arrested? Not helpful to anyone involved." They pushed off the doorframe and looked expectantly at Murphy. "I'll message my auntie and see if she's seen them anywhere in the village. With luck, we won't have to do too much searching to find our quarry."

Knowing they weren't going to budge, Murphy surrendered to the chaos. He probably wouldn't be of much use in the brewery. And if he stayed, the odds of his dad coming to check up on him were high.

That was an extra layer of chaos his day certainly didn't need.

Village gossip proved powerful once again when they learned Felicity Griffin and Marcello Lee had been spotted near one of the bed and breakfasts. Murphy wondered if they'd been staying there since the police still had the cottage cordoned off. Or, he assumed they did; he hadn't wanted to ask his cousin too many questions while George was being closely examined.

"Why don't I text Sky or Brannon?" Murphy had

known the couple who owned the bed and breakfast in question for years. He'd gone to school with Brannon. "They'll tell us if any of our potential suspects are hanging about."

"Sky's at the salon with my auntie. It's how I know they're there." Teagan grinned when he sighed. "You've no excuse not to get up. Moping about the brewery won't solve anything."

"Still texting Brannon. Maybe he's got information." Murphy allowed himself to be dragged out of his office while tapping out a message on his phone. He slipped it into his pocket when he was finished. "Are we walking or driving?"

"Walking might relieve some of your stress, but it's absolutely boiling outside. I've no interest in arriving a sweaty mess." Teagan grabbed one of the bottles of mead by the door. "Sky said not to forget we'd promised them a bottle for the BB."

"Why do you insist on calling it the BB?"

"Because it makes me laugh." Teagan headed outside, leaving him to follow after them. They smiled brightly, twirling around in the sunlight. "Let's go find a killer."

"You concern me." Murphy knew Teagan was trying to distract him from what was happening with

George. "Greatly. Did you have too much coffee this morning?"

"Rude. I had the perfect amount of coffee to prepare me to deal with the grumpiest of bears." They pointed in his direction. "I'll drive."

"I'll drive. I can't squish myself into your tiny car." Murphy stopped when his phone vibrated in his pocket. He checked to find a response to the message he'd just sent. "Brannon says Marcello Lee was gone before breakfast, but Felicity's still having a rather late brunch. If we hurry, we can have a chat with her."

Brannon was sweeping out in front of the bed and breakfast when they arrived. He waved at the two of them when they parked across the street. Murphy could see through the front windows that Felicity was enjoying her meal.

"Morning." Brannon leaned against the top of the broom. He smirked at the two of them. "Do I want to know why you're asking questions about our guests?"

"Bran." Murphy could see the mischievous twinkle in his old friend's eyes. "The police are questioning George about the murder at the cottage near his. Your guests were close friends or family to Hector Griffin. I just...."

"Want to poke your nose into another investigation and try to solve the murder yourself?" Brannon stepped to the side, nodding over his shoulder to the open door. "Go on then. She didn't seem in a hurry to leave this morning, so you've all the time in the world."

All the time in the world didn't mean Felicity would be willing to talk about her brother's murder. Murphy led the way inside. Teagan tapped his shoulder and moved in front of him; they were slightly less intimidating.

"Hello," Murphy greeted Felicity, who'd been watching since they'd entered the little dining area of the bed and breakfast. "This is Teagan. They work at the brewery with me."

"Morning." Felicity set her cup of tea down on the saucer gingerly. "Was there something I could help you with? Tim mentioned he'd gone by to apologise. Not sure why, as Marcello was the one to open his mouth to the detectives."

Murphy pulled up the image of the skincare pot from George's cottage. "Does this look familiar?"

Felicity leaned in closer to get a better glance. She reached her hand out to zoom in on the image. "Fairly sure I saw similar ones at one of the local shops. But this one specifically? No. Should it?"

Murphy considered himself somewhat decent at reading people. He didn't think she was lying about it. "You sure?"

"It's not mine. All the skincare I use comes from a Korean brand that has quite a unique branding." She handed his phone back to him. "Is this about the police inquiry?"

"Yes," Teagan answered before Murphy could think of a way to politely ask if she'd killed her brother. "Have you thought about who might have the motive to murder your brother?"

"I have." Felicity picked up her cup of tea, taking a shaky sip. "I'm convinced Tim did it. My brother was breaking up with him."

"Oh? He made it seem as though they were happy together." Murphy tried to keep his voice even and calm, hoping to coax more out of her. He thought about what Evan had heard. Gossip was never completely reliable, but someone was obviously lying. Were Hector and Tim breaking up, or were they moving in together? Was the truth somewhere in the middle? "What would he have to gain?"

"Hector was a generous soul. He had Tim in his will. If they broke up, he'd have taken him out of it almost immediately." Felicity set the cup down delicately, and she tapped a napkin to her lips. "They argued constantly. It was exhausting to be around them. Tim didn't really have a career or money, so if my brother cut him off, he'd be left with nothing."

"Was Tim staying here?" Teagan asked.

"Oh yes. He'd been in the process of moving in, but things had gotten tense between them. I think he went out for some fresh air and coffee. There's apparently a quaint little café down the street as ways. Or, maybe his guilt drove him away from me." Felicity shrugged. She seemed to be growing into this grieving sister role with each passing moment. "All I know is he left."

THIRTEEN
GEORGE

THE POLICE STATION WAS COLD, AND GEORGE wished he'd brought a jacket or jumper. The interrogation room had a strange echo-like vibe. Everything about it made him shiver uneasily.

It was alien and uncomfortable. George hated it immediately. The chair creaked when he moved even a centimetre, providing an almost torturous staccato to the whirring lights and the echo of the detectives' voices.

"Had you met Mr Griffin previously?"

"No."

"Were you aware Mr Griffin had moved into the cottage?"

"The village gossips." George sighed.

They'd asked him the same things multiple

times. Evan had already counselled him to answer honestly. He'd intervene if any questions strayed beyond what he considered normal.

So far, Evan mainly had sat back, utterly relaxed. George wished he could manage the same level of unbothered. Unfortunately, he couldn't even come close.

His skin vibrated with the anxiety in him. George wanted to go home. He wanted to go home to Bumble and his bees.

"Detective Inspector. You've already asked for and received my client's fingerprints to compare to your suspect. I'm not sure how more questioning is going to clarify anything further," Evan finally interjected into the conversation.

"I believe we can end the questions here." Elwin reached over to stop the recording. He closed the file and nodded to the other detective. "Why don't I walk you out of the station?"

"I..." George cut himself off when Evan touched his arm. "Okay."

They walked silently from the room, continuing down the hall and into bright sunshine. Evan held his shoulder, guiding him to where his car was parked. Elwin followed close behind them.

"Listen." Elwin held a hand up when Evan went

to interrupt. "Off the record. The pot of cream appears to have been bought locally by someone from the village. Not you. We checked. We're having the contents analysed, but the results could take days. I've a sneaking suspicion that the lab won't find any venom in it. I've a feeling it's not connected to the murder."

"Then how?"

"Have you considered your cousin might have left it?" Elwin took a step closer to them, dropping his voice even lower. "We have to ask uncomfortable questions and follow the evidence, but no one believes you did anything to Hector Griffin. I certainly don't. You're a good, gentle soul. Please resist the urge to investigate."

It was comforting to know at least one of the detectives didn't believe he'd been involved in a murder. However, George wasn't sure he'd be able to fully relax until the murderer had been caught. There were too many unanswered questions.

Once in the safety of Evan's vehicle, George reached for his backpack. He found his headphones and shoved them on his head, flicking the switch for the noise-cancellation. They offered a blessed buffer from the ambient noise around him.

Arriving at the cottage, Evan sent him inside. He promised to give Murphy and everyone else an update. George stared at the front of his home for several minutes after his attorney drove off.

His eyes followed the lines of ivy creeping up the stone. It gave him something to focus on: counting the endless leaves. The almost hypnotic nature of the meaningless task allowed him to finally find the energy to head into the cottage.

"Beta." His father saw him first when he stepped into the living room. He frowned when George simply stared at him. His gaze flicked up to the headphones. "Ah. Okay."

Duncan had been sitting on the couch with Bumble in his lap. He gently set the pug onto the floor, who immediately trotted over to George. "How about we spend some time with Margo down the lane? Give you a few hours to yourself? I'll give our Paddington a call. Make sure he knows you're all right and need a little quiet to recover."

George could only nod in agreement. He absently bent down to lift Bumble into his arms. Words felt like far too much of an effort at the moment.

"Beta?" His father stepped closer and placed a

soft kiss on his forehead. "Send me a text message when you're ready for something to eat, okay? We'll bring your favourites."

Before leaving him to his own devices, his father made a mug of one of his non-caffeinated chai blends. He added milk and put several biscuits on a plate, setting both on the coffee table. George waited until they'd left to move over to the couch, sinking down and groaning loudly.

Being in his own cottage had never felt so good. George closed his eyes, enjoying the muffled sound of the birds through the open window behind him and Bumble snuffling in his lap. He tried to keep from replaying the conversation with the police in his mind.

It was hard not to think of a million different ways their questions could've been answered. George knew those thoughts wouldn't help in the long run. The conversation had ended. He had no way to go back and change things.

On a whim, George went into the small loo off the kitchen. He inspected the cabinet with fresh eyes. Now he knew Felicity likely hadn't planted the pot; he wondered who had left it.

A container with a similar label caught his attention. It had gotten shoved behind a container of cotton buds. He flipped the tube lid open, giving it a tentative whiff.

No smell of honey, though venom wouldn't even remotely be similar. He carefully inspected the ingredients to find them devoid of anything bee-related. Nevertheless, the scent tugged on his memories.

Auntie Valerie.

Rushing back into the living room, George found his phone where he'd tossed it to the side. He texted his auntie Valerie a photo of the little tube of fancy sunscreen. *Formulated for the face? What does that even mean? Is face skin different from everywhere else?*

Auntie Valerie was his mum's sister. She lived in Edinburgh but had been to visit him several times. The scent of the sunscreen had reminded him of her for some reason.

After a few minutes, Valerie responded to his message, confirming the tube and the eye cream belonged to her. He breathed a sigh of relief. Felicity hadn't been attempting to frame him for murder.

Or, at least, she hadn't done it with eye cream, if she did it at all. It didn't explain why she'd been snooping around his cottage. George wondered if maybe she was just an incredibly nosy person.

Returning to the couch, George tried to relax by counting out his breaths in sets of four. In, hold, out, hold. He couldn't. Something about the interrogation had put him on edge more than he'd expected.

Of the three suspects, George was leaning towards the boyfriend. Tim Frederick. He'd been so eager to apologise for pointing the police in his direction. But had he been too apologetic?

Too eager?

George tried to push the mystery out of his mind. The detectives could handle the investigation. It wasn't his job, but he kept returning to one fact. *Why fill a house with bees?*

The odds of Hector Griffin being stung weren't as high as one might imagine. If he walked into a cottage to find bees, surely he'd have immediately left. None of it made sense.

His phone beeped a few times with new messages. George silenced it. He took several minutes to simply sit and enjoy the breeze coming through the window.

Bumble broke his calm. He snorted loudly, then slowly shifted up, pawing at the edge of the sofa.

George set him down and got up to open the back door, allowing him into the garden.

"What are we going to do, Bumble?" George kept an eye on the pug who trundled around the garden, inspecting flowers and hunting for butterflies. "Yes, following the pollinators seems like an excellent plan."

As each minute passed, George allowed the tension to bleed away. Being in the garden always had that effect on him. He stretched out in the grass and watched the clouds floating by; he chuckled when Bumble came over to sit next to his head.

"Pretty sure that one looks like you." George pointed to one of the fluffy clouds. Bumble flopped down on his belly, utterly unimpressed. "Are you missing your best friend? Should we go see how Treacle is appreciating the chaos of Abba and *his* best mate, Duncan?"

At Treacle's name, Bumble immediately clambered back up. He wiggled around exactly and licked George's face until he had to sit up. It was a clear and obvious yes.

"All right, give me a moment." George did a quick perusal around the garden, making sure nothing needed his immediate attention. He used his phone to jot down a few notes about stray weeds he'd take care of later. "You ready? Maybe we should bring some of the honey saffron syrup I made. I bet Abba would make pancakes for us."

His father's pancakes were the best ones, in his opinion, and a comfort food from his childhood. He'd gone through months of eating nothing but them for breakfast. Something his parents had gone along with to help make his life easier.

They'd always done that. Going out of their way to adjust to whatever would make his passage in the world less difficult. George knew he'd been very, very lucky to have patient and loving parents like his.

George led Bumble back into the cottage. He locked up the back, picked up his backpack and keys, and made his way to the front door. He opened it and froze when he spotted Marcello Lee with his fist raised, ready to knock. "Hello."

"Could we have a chat?"

"Why?" George wasn't anxious to let the man into his cottage for a second time. "Not sure you should be here."

"I think Felicity killed her brother—and I'm afraid I'm next on her list." Marcello peered around as if he expected her to pop out of the hedge. "She'd have a controlling interest in the company without me since I believe she'll inherit Hector's portion."

"Ah."

"May I come in?"

George hesitated before finally stepping back. "Come on. I'll put the kettle on for tea."

FOURTEEN

MURPHY

"Why don't we see if we can find Tim Frederick? I'd love to know what he thinks of Felicity's accusations." Murphy had gotten a text from his father about George returning from the interrogation and needing some peace and quiet. He'd sent a quick message to his boyfriend, telling him to let him know if he needed anything at all. "Maybe he'll be more open to talking with us."

"Didn't Detective Constable Smith tell you to stay out of the inquiry?" Teagan followed him down the pavement towards one of the cafés in the village. "Do you think Tim did it?"

"I think Felicity Griffin very much wants us to believe Tim did it. Not sure she's being completely

honest with us. I've no idea." Murphy thought she'd pushed the angle of Hector's estate a little too aggressively, particularly given they were complete strangers. "Was she too eager to tell us intimate details of their lives?"

"Maybe. We did ask." Teagan caught his arm when he went to cross the street. "Isn't that him?"

Murphy followed their gaze further down the lane until he spotted a familiar figure outside of the bookshop. "It is. Why don't we invite him for a coffee? Have a little casual conversation?"

"A casual conversation where we accuse him of murdering his boyfriend." Teagan chuckled. They made their way to where Tim was perusing a bookshelf outside the shop. "Hello."

"Hello?" He frowned at them in confusion before spotting Murphy. "Oh. You. What do you want?"

Murphy was surprised at the slight hostility in the man's voice. He'd seemed friendly enough when he'd visited the cottage. What had changed? "How are you enjoying Dufftown so far?"

"It's nice enough. A good selection of books, at least." Tim held up the ones in his hand. "I've already found a few to take home with me."

"Planning on leaving?"

"Soon. I've no reason to stay. Small village life really isn't my style." Tim shrugged. He picked up another book, making a show of inspecting the cover for longer than really necessary. "I'm waiting for the police to release poor Hector back to us."

"Are you coordinating with his sister about the funeral?" Teagan slipped the question casually into the conversation. They showed no signs of being overly interested in the response. "Were you planning to have it here or take him—"

"Those are private decisions made by the family." Tim cut them off. He slammed the book shut that he'd been perusing. "I'm not privy to any of it."

"Felicity mentioned you and Hector had been in the process of breaking up." Murphy decided if the conversation was getting derailed, he might as well delve into another touchy subject. "That you were arguing?"

"What? No. We... every couple has arguments. It wasn't anything new or extreme. And how would she know? She had no relationship with her brother aside from asking him for money." Tim spun towards them. He clutched the books to his chest and glared at both of them. "I didn't kill him. I loved him. If anyone had a motive, it was Marcello."

"Oh? Really?" Murphy was intrigued. Hector's friends and family certainly seemed eager to point the finger at one another. "Weren't they business partners?"

"Marcello wanted to sell the company. They had a massive offer, but Hector refused to consider it. Instead, he planned to move everything to a new warehouse or something. I didn't quite hear all of it. He didn't talk business with me often. I picked up bits and pieces when he was on the phone." Tim lifted his chin up, glowering at both of them. "We were happy."

"Were you?"

"Every couple has their arguments. It doesn't mean our relationship was over." Tim shifted the books over to one arm and scrubbed at a few stray tears that had slipped down his cheeks. "I loved him. I'd have put up with a lot to stay with him. We were just having a little rough patch."

"How rough?" Teagan prompted gently after a moment.

"Not sure that's any of your business. I didn't kill him. I couldn't have. I wasn't anywhere near the cottage when he died—and I certainly didn't go about collecting bees." Tim set the stack of books down on the table, clearly growing tired of holding them. "All I know is Marcello and Hector rowed about selling the business. He likes to gamble, think he might've needed the money."

"Hector?"

"No, Marcello. He's always going on holidays for big poker tournaments, though Felicity might know more. They were quite cosy together for years. I never liked the man." Tim adjusted his shirt, brushing it down and clearing his throat a few times. He reached out to pick up the books once again. "I think I've chatted enough to satisfy your salient curiosity. Sod off and leave me alone."

Murphy smothered down an urge to chuckle at how Tim marched into the bookshop, practically slamming the door behind him. "Well, he told us."

"Think he did it?" Teagan asked.

"I don't, actually. I think his grief is genuine. Not that a killer can't experience sadness over the death of their victim. But I'm not sure he had it in him to murder Hector." Murphy watched through the shop window while Tim seemed to be struggling to *not* glance in their direction. "Come on. Why don't we see what Felicity has to say for herself? I know we just spoke with her, but I've got more questions. I'm curious about how cosy she was with Marcello. She was eager to shove us in this direction—maybe it was misdirection."

Leaving the vehicle parked in the village, they decided to walk the short distance back to the bed and breakfast. They both had questions for Felicity. Though Murphy did wonder how angry the detectives would be when they discovered his snooping into the inquiry.

With George potentially being dragged into the case, Murphy couldn't sit back and do nothing. He had to try. If nothing else, it distracted him from bombarding his boyfriend with messages.

George needed calm, not an endless stream of texts asking how he was doing. Murphy figured trying to find answers was a better use of his time. He hoped.

Brannon had moved his cleaning inside when they arrived back at the bed and breakfast. He had a vacuum in his hand instead of a broom. Murphy whistled sharply to catch his attention over the high-pitched whine.

"Twice in one day? Looking for my guests again?" Brannon propped the vacuum hose against his leg. "You've missed Felicity if she's who you're after. She left a few minutes after you. Grabbed all her bags, practically threw the keys in my face, and vanished. I don't think she even finished her breakfast."

"Really? How odd." Teagan exchanged a worried glance with Murphy. "Did she say anything at all?"

"I heard her on the phone, talking to one of the detectives. Maybe Elwin? She was asking if they'd detained George. Oi. Where are you running off to now?" Brannon rushed out of the front door after them. "Paddy? You okay?"

"Call you later." Murphy fumbled with his keys, cursing when they slipped through his fingers. Something wasn't right. Why had she run off all of a sudden? He snatched them off the ground, regretting not just driving back to the bed and breakfast from the bookshop to begin with. They were wasting precious time. "You call Elwin. I'm going to try to get George on the phone."

"It might be nothing."

"Probably is. But I can't shake this nagging feeling he's in danger. And I'm not betting his life on my being paranoid. Bugger." Murphy cursed loudly when he hit the wrong contact and wound up dialling his father, who picked up on the second ring. "Shite."

"Watch your language, lad. What's the trouble?"

"Think something might be wrong with George." Murphy was out of breath by the time they arrived at his vehicle. Nevertheless, he managed to get the doors open without dropping his keys this time. "Can you and Rishi swing around to check on him? We're on our way. And I'm calling Sarah and Elwin as soon as you hang up."

His father disconnected without even saying goodbye. Murphy heard Teagan shouting at who he thought might be one of the detectives about their concerns, so he decided not to add his own call to the chaos. He focused on driving through the village as quickly but safely as possible.

Teagan finally finished their call. They grunted when Murphy took a corner too quickly. "Easy, Paddy. Getting us killed in a ditch won't help George."

"Did you get Elwin?"

"He's questioning a suspect." Teagan still had their phone out and was furiously typing out a message. "Your cousin's in with him. The absolute plonker who answered refused to interrupt them but did 'take the message to inform them when they've finished.' How is that even helpful at all?"

"Who are you messaging?" Murphy slammed on

the brakes, throwing an arm out to protect Teagan. "Move, you furry little arses."

Teagan snickered despite the tension. "Sheep move on their own schedule, not ours."

"Fancy mutton for dinner?"

"Paddington."

FIFTEEN
GEORGE

From outside in the garden, George heard his phone going off inside the cottage. He'd made tea for his guest, and they'd gone out to enjoy the summer weather. It would be rude to abruptly end the conversation, but he was dying to know who kept calling him.

"I don't know what Felicity was thinking. She's made a mess of everything and run off as always. Stupid woman." Marcello had been ranting about Felicity Griffin almost since he sat down. "Can you believe her?"

"I... no?" George grew increasingly uneasy about being stuck having tea with Marcello. He didn't understand why the man had sought him out. "I

don't know her, so I can't say if she's behaving out of the ordinary. Has she gone somewhere?"

"She's catching a flight to London to speak with Hector's solicitor. Not that it'll do her any good. Her brother didn't leave the business in her incapable hands." Marcello calmly sipped his tea, setting the cup back on the table. "I have controlling interest once again, as I should've done all along."

"Oh?"

"It was my idea."

"Right." George had no idea where the conversation was going. He tried to nod in all the appropriate places. At the same time, Marcello continued his verbal vomiting about his business prowess and overall brilliance. "I'm not trying to be rude, but why exactly are you here?"

"The police released you."

"Yes?" George hadn't meant it to come out in such a questioning tone. He wondered how Marcello had even heard, granted village gossip travelled like lightning. "Why?"

"Thought they'd arrest you."

"For what? I haven't done anything. They asked questions. I answered." George reached down to lift Bumble into his arms. His anxiety was starting to spark. All the relaxation work from earlier was quickly being undone. "There's nothing connecting me to your friend's murder besides a short interaction and bees."

It seemed wise not to prod the man too much, so George didn't mention the bees hadn't stung Hector. The police hadn't yet determined where or if he'd come in contact with the venom. If that was what had triggered his allergic reaction. All he knew was it had nothing at all to do with him.

Bumble growled when Marcello continued to speak. It reminded George of a few days prior when he'd been so agitated in the garden. He frowned, wondering if he finally had an answer to who'd been trespassing at the hives.

His phone went off once again. George bent forward to set Bumble gently on the ground. He stuck close instead of trundling off into the garden.

"Do you mind? I should answer." George went to move, but Marcello's hand shot out, catching him by the wrist. "What—"

"The police will start suspecting me sooner or later." Marcello pulled a wicked-looking knife out underneath his jacket and balanced it on his knee. "Found this amongst Hector's things. It belonged to their father, I think. Something he picked up on his travels. Maybe they'll believe Felicity did it."

"Pardon?"

"I'm going to have to kill you."

"To avoid the police? Do you realise how daft you sound? The police might potentially suspect me of murder, so I'll just skip along and kill another person. There's no two-for-one deal on death." George yanked his arm out of Marcello's wrist. He tried to step back and put a little distance between them. "If they don't suspect you now, they certainly will if you stab me."

"A risk I'll have to take." Marcello reached out for the knife. He inspected it briefly while keeping his eye on George. "You were such a convenient person to blame for the murder. All those bees. It should've been easy for him to be stung. I tried one in his bedroom the first time. The second attempt was several in his car, but it didn't work. He panicked and managed to get away without being stung. I slipped four or five into the cottage, but again it failed."

"You're why he thought I was setting my bees on him." George couldn't believe his ears. "I'm not surprised he came screaming to my door if he thought bees were somehow finding their way into his cottage."

To his complete dismay, Marcello laughed. George didn't get the joke. None of it was humorous.

A cruel joke followed up with murderous intent. George found himself feeling even more sympathy for Hector Griffin. He probably felt like he was losing his mind when bees reappeared despite his best attempts to keep them out of his cottage.

"What did you do once the bees didn't work?" George crept slowly towards the cottage door. He hoped to put some space between himself and the homicidal villain with his dagger. "They don't sting on command."

"I'm aware." Marcello rose from the chair. He shifted the knife from one hand to the other. "You can buy venom. We had some come through our shipping company. It was nothing at all to make a portion of the shipment disappear."

As Marcello explained how he'd put venom in everything he could think of, George continued to inch his way towards the cottage. He didn't know if he'd manage to get inside and lock the door. It was going to be a close thing.

"What about the bees?"

"Had a bunch shipped to me. It was easy to capture one or two, but I wanted to fill the cottage after I was sure he was dead. I figured maybe they'd sting him a few times. Then the police would realise he'd gone into anaphylactic shock and assume the bees had done it." Marcello suddenly noticed how close George was to reaching the door. "I wouldn't do that if I were you. There's nowhere to hide."

Before George could respond, Marcello lunged towards him. He had a second to react, flinging himself to the right on top of the lavender patch. It made for a floral landing; puffs of purple flew up around him.

Shite.

Purple shite.

Rolling out of the way, George narrowly avoided being grabbed or stabbed. He shuffled backwards, still on his hands and knees. As Marcello scrambled after him, George tried to get to his feet and run.

George didn't have time to mourn the section of his garden getting laid to waste in the scramble. Instead, he deftly darted out of the way of Marcello's reaching arm, darting down to grab Bumble and legged it for the gate. *Shite. Shite. Shite.*

"Beta?"

"Run," George shouted when he spotted his father and Duncan walking up the lane towards him. "Run. He's got a knife."

They didn't run.

They kept coming towards him.

George clutched Bumble tightly in his arms, ignoring his squirming to get down. "He... has... a knife."

"Breathe, beta. Breathe." His father placed a hand on his shoulder. He peered around George towards the cottage. "He's gone."

George bent his head forward to rest against his father's arm. He took great heaving breaths, trying to find some semblance of calm. "He had a knife."

"I'm calling Sarah." Duncan gently took Bumble from him. He had his phone in his other hand. "I'll take your wee pug. Just calm yourself right down. Everything's okay."

"I crushed my lavender."

"Well, as things go, I'd rather you crush your lavender than the life be crushed out of you." His father kept an arm tightly around his shoulders. "Just keep taking those slow breaths. I don't see him anywhere. He probably caught sight of us and didn't like his odds against the three of us."

George noticed Murphy's vehicle coming flying down the lane towards them. He skidded to a stop and leapt out with Teagan close behind. "I'm okay."

Murphy rushed up to him. He didn't even notice

their fathers or anyone else as he dragged George into a crushing embrace. "You're all right?"

"I've had better days, but I'll live. Just a few scratches and bruises from where I fell into the lavender." George hated that he'd wrecked part of his garden. "It was Marcello Lee."

SIXTEEN

MURPHY

IT TOOK A FEW MINUTES FOR GEORGE TO STOP feeling like a weak breeze might knock him over. Murphy kept an arm around him and an eye out for Marcello to reappear. They huddled in the lane outside the cottage, waiting for the police to arrive.

"We should go check things out." His dad piped up after a minute or two. "Your cousin Sarah claims they're on their way. Nothing stopping us from going into the cottage."

"Da." Murphy mentally sent up a prayer to the universe for the police to hurry up. If they decided to investigate the cottage, Duncan and Rishi would be impossible to corral. He couldn't say anything; he'd spent far too much time poking into the inquiry. "We should wait for Sarah and Elwin."

"He might escape." Rishi leapt into the conversation, eager to back up his partner in crime. "We'll just peer over the fence to see if he's in the garden."

"Abba." George tried to step in and calm them both down. "It's technically a crime scene. I'd rather not muck it up any further than it has been."

"Where's your sense of adventure?" Rishi came over and patted his hands on George's cheeks, ignoring his son's groan of embarrassment. "You're alive. Your Bumble is alive. Now we must hunt the man who threatened you."

"Abba," George repeated. He appeared to be torn between laughing and groaning. "I'll call Mum."

"This is how you treat me?"

George covered his face with his hand. "This is serious, Abba. You can't go traipsing around after a knife-wielding killer."

"Why?" Rishi glanced over at Duncan. "I've seen worse."

"Where?"

"Well, I...." Rishi trailed off when they finally heard police sirens in the distance. "Ah, well. Too late."

While George stared up at the sky, probably begging for strength to deal with his father, Murphy watched as multiple vehicles came racing down the lane. He spotted Elwin and Sarah in the lead. They quickly jogged over to the little group outside of the cottage.

"Where are they?" Elwin asked immediately.

"Marcello Lee confessed to killing Hector Griffin before attempting to stab me with a knife. I ran. No idea where he went. I thought he was following me." George spoke so quickly that his words almost ran together. He barely took a breath while giving the detectives the information. "He bought venom. He said he bought venom. Put it in everything of Hector's."

"Okay." Elwin held a hand up to stop George before he could continue. "Do you have your keys?"

George immediately shook his head. "In the cottage."

"Fine. That's fine. Why don't all of you head to Margo's down the lane? It's better than lingering out here and safer since we have no idea where Marcello Lee has gone." Sarah stepped up beside her partner. "We'll take it from here."

The police waited until they began moving towards Margo's to head for the cottage. Murphy kept glancing over his shoulder, but they soon disappeared from view. He didn't believe they were going to find Marcello.

Once Marcello's prey had escaped, the man would surely bolt himself. He couldn't be foolish enough to remain behind. It made Murphy uneasy, wondering where he could've gone.

Would he try to finish the job? Or take the wiser course and flee the village? Given the money at his disposal, Murphy could see Marcello attempting to leave the country if he were smart.

Marcello hadn't proven himself to be overly clever. The method of murder was brilliant, but he'd made loads of mistakes. Murphy wondered if he'd fallen victim to the classic issue of believing himself to be the most intelligent person in the room.

There was a vast difference between being clever and *believing* oneself to be smart. Marcello seemed more the latter than the former. Time, Murphy supposed, would tell.

"Paddy?"

Murphy turned back from where he'd stopped to glance towards the cottage. Their dads had continued on to Margo's ahead of them. "Yeah?"

"Are we murder magnets now? Are we just going to keep stumbling into police inquiries? I don't like this new development." George closed the distance between them. He slid an arm around Murphy's waist so he could lean against him. "I've ruined half of my lavender patch."

"We can replant it. You are more important than the lavender. You're not as easy to replace. We can't find 'George' bulbs at a gardening shop." Murphy was relieved to hear a snicker from his boyfriend. He'd been too quiet on the walk to Margo's. "We can't shove you feet first into the soil and pour water over your head."

"You could try." George gave another quiet chuckle. "Lavender doesn't have bulbs. It grows from seeds. Technically, it's probably easiest to propagate them from cuttings."

"Not all of us have a wealth of plant knowledge shoved into our noggin, Buzz." Murphy draped his arm lightly across George's shoulders. "Did you get hurt in all this tumbling amongst the flora and fauna?"

"Technically...."

"Buzz." Murphy sent a withering look at George, who smiled. "Were you hurt?"

"Probably have a few bruises." George lifted his arm, shoving his sleeve up to reveal a long scrape. "This is the sum total of my injuries. Just a long scratch."

Murphy caught his wrist, holding it while he inspected the scratch. "I think you'll live."

George rolled his eyes when Murphy kissed the scratch. He shoved his face away. "Don't be weird."

"Romantic."

"Weird," George retorted. "Do you think they'll find him?"

"At your cottage? No. He'd be daft to remain after you escaped. You'd obviously call for help, so staying would increase the odds of being captured." Murphy pulled him off to the side when another police car came up the lane behind them. It was followed by a second and then a third. "Seems they've called for backup."

"Maybe they found him." George didn't sound overly hopeful.

"Or they want help searching for him in the wilds beyond your cottage." Murphy thought it more likely they'd decided to see if he'd gone to ground in the nearby countryside. "

"Hardly the wilds." George peered around him when they heard yet another car coming up the lane. "How much help do they need?"

"He's got several minutes on them. And there are a lot of hedges and fields to cover." Murphy figured Marcello had fled on foot. They'd have seen him if he'd left in his vehicle. "I'm sure we'll find out what's going on eventually."

Nodding in response, George settled into silence beside him. He shivered a little despite the sun above them. Murphy shifted his hold so he had both arms wrapped around him, hoping to provide comfort and warmth.

The quiet gave him plenty of time to think about how wrong he'd been about Felicity. He'd genuinely thought she was involved. It was a surprise to find she hadn't been.

"Why don't we go inside and get some tea?"

George shook his head. "I want to see if anything happens."

"Think we might be in for a long wait." Murphy was tempted to move back towards the cottage for a closer look, even if it might make their detective friends a little irate. "We could—"

"Walk closer to check for my keys that I might've dropped?" George smiled up at him.

"You said you'd left them in the cottage."

"Entirely possible they magically made it into my pocket, then fell out." George moved out of Murphy's embrace. He reached down to take his hand instead. "I've got to do something. I feel simultaneously like a lorry ran over me, but also that I've drunk the strongest espresso in the history of espressos."

"Fear and adrenaline will do that to a person." Murphy wondered if he might take George into Margo's for tea and maybe something sweet to nibble. "Why don't we ensure our dads aren't driving your poor cousin batty?"

Instead of answering, George walked forward down the lane. Murphy followed with him. His hand was still held tightly.

Aside from the massive number of police vehicles, Murphy saw no sign of activity at the cottage. No one stood outside or was visible through the front windows.

"We shouldn't go inside." George's statement sounded far more like a question. "Right? We shouldn't."

"I imagine our attorney would advise against it." Murphy noticed that the thought didn't stop either of them from inching forward.

"And your cousin, the detective, who's already been quite cross with us. She'd probably say this was a bad idea." George took another step in the direction of his cottage. "Detective Constable Smith would probably *advise* against it as well. We might give them a complex."

"Maybe they'll start a support group." Murphy froze when they noticed movement in the front windows—one of the local police constables immediately waved at them to stop. "We've been spotted."

"Whatever gave you that idea?" George twisted around to face in the opposite direction. He took a calm, measured breath while glancing across the valley. His home was situated for a perfect view down into the village. "I don't want this to ruin how I feel about my cottage."

"Why should it?"

"Marcello came into my home."

"Well, since you invited him. Maybe don't go inviting any more murderers?" Murphy teased, trying to lighten the mood. They'd both had a scare, but dwelling on it wouldn't help ease their fears. He slipped his arm around George again, drawing him into his side. "This is an anomaly. Your cottage is perfectly safe."

"Aside from the man wielding a knife."

"Well, nowhere is perfect. We'll have the locks changed." Murphy peered over his shoulder when he heard the cottage door open. Elwin appeared a moment later, frowning in their direction. "It appears we're about to be summoned. We should probably send Evan a message."

"Brilliant."

Murphy could appreciate the slight hint of dread in George's voice. "At least they can't accuse either of us this time around. They've got the killer red-handed. Or maybe not quite, but hopefully the investigation will find all the evidence they need."

"Red-handed. Why is that a phrase? Marcello's hands weren't red at all. Maybe pinkish? Or salmon? Maybe a light rose or even an off-white?" George pondered the question for a while longer, going on about the hue of skin tone. "You're laughing at me."

"Not exactly," Murphy grunted when George elbowed him in the side. "I had no idea you knew so many shades of pink."

"Hilarious," George huffed. "You've successfully managed to distract from my earlier emotional blip."

"Emotional blip?"

Before George could answer, Elwin shouted for their attention. He remained at the front of the cottage, motioning for them to join him. Murphy looked to his boyfriend, who simply shrugged.

What else could they do? They'd made the decision to ignore the advice to go to Margo's. They might as well face whatever Elwin wanted to say to them.

"This is *not* Margo's cottage," Elwin hissed at

them. He folded his arms across his chest, glowering at the two of them. "We gave very specific instructions."

"We went. We saw. We returned. What's the Latin for that?" Murphy had a smidge of sympathy for Elwin. But it wasn't as if they were trying to make his job more difficult. They'd remained outside, after all. "Did you find him?"

"Not yet. He appears to have fled through the garden towards Hector Griffin's cottage. We're attempting to follow his trail from there. I'd appreciate it if you returned to Margo's for your safety. Please." Elwin reached into his pocket and pulled out George's keys. "We found this by the front door. When we're finished, I'll lock up and bring these back to you."

Murphy managed a nod before Elwin spun around and reentered the cottage, shutting the door in their faces. "So much for that plan."

"Off to Margo's?"

"Off to Margo's."

SEVENTEEN
GEORGE

On the walk back to Margo's, George eased his phone out of his pocket. He did a search for the phrase "red-handed." His brain had decided to latch onto it as a distraction from everything else.

"Easy there, Buzz." Murphy caught him by the arm when he stumbled over a pebble. "Maybe don't read and walk?"

"Red-handed apparently comes from an old fifteenth-century Scottish law. Who knew? It quite literally refers to a murderer being caught with blood on their hands." George highlighted information from the *Encyclopedia of Word and Phrase Origins*. He wanted to do more research later. "Sir Walter Scott had the first use in Ivanhoe in the 1800s."

Murphy guided him around another rough patch

before they finally arrived at Margo's. "Surprised Treacle and Bumble aren't here to greet us."

"Me too." George pocketed his phone. "I could use tea and a biscuit or five."

Finding the front door open, George made his way inside. He froze when he came to the end of the hall, causing Murphy to bump into him. They spotted Marcello Lee tied to a kitchen chair by dog leads.

"What the actual—" George didn't know how to process what he was seeing. The window of the back door was shattered. He could hear Treacle and Bumble whining from upstairs, so Margo had clearly locked them away in a bedroom. "Has anyone called the police?"

"I just spoke with Sarah. They'll be here in a few moments, I imagine." Duncan waved his phone as if to prove it. "Not sure she believed me at first until I sent her a photo."

"Sent her a photo," George repeated. He parsed the words out in his mind and still found himself stunned. "You messaged Sarah. Detective Constable Baird. An officer of the law. You messaged her a photo of a suspected murderer tied to a chair with dog leads."

"Yes." Duncan smiled broadly, waving a hand

towards Marcello. "He threatened Margo with a knife. This was mild in comparison."

"Right. Okay. Right." George felt like his brain was in desperate need of a reboot. He couldn't quite get past the absurdity of the moment. His father stood on Marcello's other side, keeping a close eye on the man. "I am going to stand over there far away from the impact zone when the detectives arrive because they're not going to be pleased."

Skirting around the madness in the living room, George stepped into the kitchen. He was immediately handed a mug of tea from Margo, who sipped from her own cup. She winked at him, obviously amused.

"Sarah's not going to find this funny." George kept his voice down.

"Sarah rarely finds anything we do funny. She'll survive. Besides, have you ever attempted to get Rishi Sheth or Duncan Baird to behave themselves when they're together? It's impossible." Margo set her mug on the counter behind her. "Treacle and Bumble are upstairs in my bedroom, if you're wondering. They've snacks, water, and all the blankets in the world. I didn't want them underfoot with all the chaos."

"You're calmer than I was." George hadn't quite

recovered from his own close encounter with Marcello's knife. "My heart's still racing a little."

"That's why I've given you some of the chamomile and lavender tea you made for me. Something to serve the nerves. It's what I'm drinking as well. I added a little of the lemon-infused honey." She shifted closer to him. "You all right? Any injuries? Did they call an ambulance for you?"

"Just a scrape and a few bruises from crashing into my lavender." George showed her the long scratch on his forearm. "It's not even bleeding. I'm fine. A bit shaken but all right."

It was only a few minutes before the front door practically crashed open. The police rushed into the cottage. George wondered what they'd been expecting because the four seemed stunned by what they saw.

Hadn't Duncan mentioned sending Sarah a photo?

Calm was restored when Sarah and Elwin joined the now-crowded group in the cottage. Once they'd freed Marcello of the dog leads, he was handcuffed and led away by the constables. The detectives remained behind.

Sarah held up a hand when everyone went to

speak at once. "Stop. Please. Margo? Why don't you tell us what happened?"

While Margo explained Marcello showing up in her garden, George remained in the kitchen, where Murphy joined him. They shared his mug of tea while listening in on the conversation. It was brief; he had no doubts the detectives would want all of them to give their statements individually in more detail later.

"He didn't make any confessions once we had him tied up." Duncan shrugged.

"Your da is not even remotely bothered by all of this," George whispered to Murphy. "Pretty sure both our fathers think this is some grand adventure. We're never going to hear the end of this."

"Every holiday meal. I can hear them now. Remember the time we single-handedly stopped a deadly killer? He was armed to the teeth but no match for us." Murphy chuckled under his breath. "It'll be like the fishing trip all over again when they came back claiming to have caught a shark."

George brought both of his hands up to measure a ridiculous distance. "It was this big."

"Bigger."

"And where were you when all of this was

happening?" Elwin had stepped away from Sarah and joined them in the kitchen.

"Outside. Remember? We went for a stroll." Murphy handed the mug of tea back to George, who took a sip before setting it down on the counter. "We can't be roped into being blamed for this. Talk to my da and his."

"I'll leave that to Sarah. She's better equipped." Elwin winked at them. He pretended to jot down a few things in his notebook while talking to them. "Anything to add to the conversation?"

"Nothing at all." George wanted to be back in his cottage with Bumble and Murphy. He'd had enough of Marcello Lee and anything connected to him. "Can I go home? Did he wreck it?"

"There's damage to one of the hedges along the east side of your garden and the lavender patch. Nothing else appears harmed. Not sure he ever entered the cottage, to be honest. We didn't find any sign of him. Once we've gotten the brief notes from everyone's statements, you can go home." Elwin patted him lightly on the shoulder. "Just... maybe stop inviting strangers into your cottage? For my sake and yours. For everyone's."

"Never inviting anyone into my cottage ever again." George ignored Murphy's laughing beside him. "Maybe I should put a sign? A Not Welcome sign?"

"I don't think you have to take drastic measures." Elwin was definitely struggling not to grin at him. "Just be more careful when there's a killer on the loose."

"I'll make you a giant NO sign. You can hold it up if strangers come to your door," Margo promised as she joined them in the kitchen. "Why don't I make us all another batch of tea?"

"None for us. We've got a suspect to question. We'll want official statements from you three at the station later." Susan pointed to Rishi, Duncan, and Margo. "Just try to stay out of trouble. Please. I'm begging all of you."

"We'll do our level best to avoid any random killer showing up at our door. Not sure what we can do if they barge in through the garden." Duncan Baird seemed impervious to his niece's glowering. "Good luck with your questioning, Detectives. We have complete faith in your abilities."

Unable to tune them out, George decided he'd had enough chaos and conversation. He weaved his way through everyone gathered and continued to Margo's bedroom. Treacle and Bumble immediately rushed over to him, wiggling their little bodies around him.

"Hello, you two. Were you tired of being all cooped up by yourself? Missing all the excitement?" George carefully continued further into the room. He sank onto the plush rug and leaned against Margo's bed. The two pups immediately clambered into his lap. Treacle managed to climb up to sit on his shoulder. "All right, Treacle. Easy there. You're not a mountain goat."

For the first time in days, George managed to take a deep, calming breath. They'd caught the killer. And it wasn't him. The police had no reason to suspect him of anything at all.

Despite Evan's reassurances, George couldn't shake off his anxiety over being questioned. He could have been arrested. It happened all the time. He'd read many news articles about people being arrested for crimes they hadn't committed.

Treacle sniffed at his ear before giving George a few quick licks. He scrambled back down his chest with all the grace of a baby giraffe, dropping on top of Bumble, who grunted. It made him laugh when they finally wound up cuddling together in his lap, giving equally dramatic sighs.

He dropped his head back against the mattress

and closed his eyes. "What do you think, Bumble? Strangest summer ever?"

Bumble didn't answer, but there was a knock on the door. George sighed. He didn't want company, but it wasn't his cottage, so he told them to come in.

The door cracked open enough for Murphy to poke his head inside. Bumble perked up. He shifted his head up and rested it on top of Treacle's.

"Found an oasis of calm, have you?" Murphy came over to crouch in front of him. "Everything all right?"

"Just feel like an elastic band stretched too far, and my brain is about to snap." George lifted his head up when Murphy crouched in front of him. "Me and the pups have definitely seen enough excitement for one day."

"How about I walk you back to your cottage? Margo can distract our dads and keep them out of trouble for the rest of the day. Are you hungry? I can whip something up or grab a takeaway." Murphy scratched Bumble's ear, then gently placed his hand on George's shoulder. "How about a pizza? A pizza and some mead fresh from the brewery? I'm sure Teagan wouldn't mind playing delivery driver for us. They're already upset to have missed all the excitement."

"Excitement?" George couldn't help raising an eyebrow. "Not sure it's the word I'd use."

"Maybe, but it's not every day your father ties a murderer to a chair." Murphy gave his shoulder a gentle squeeze. "Come on. You'll be more comfortable in your own space. And I'm sure you're itching to make sure Marcello didn't muck up your cottage."

By some miracle, Margo had convinced both of their dads to go into the village on a shop run. She sent George home with a basket of freshly baked treats. Something she'd done all afternoon to work through her anxiety.

"Give me a text later, will you? Are you still planning to go to the Highland Games on the weekend?" Margo added one last packet of biscuits to the basket in his arms. "We can walk together with the pups."

George had forgotten all about the upcoming Highland Games. It was something Murphy took part in each year. He made a fine figure in his kilt, launching heavy objects across a field. "Of course, I wouldn't miss it."

"A little thing like murder shouldn't dampen your enjoyment." Margo frowned. "I could've put that better."

"Probably."

EIGHTEEN

MURPHY

The past few days had been eventful, with the police murder inquiry finally wrapping up. Murphy had been caught up in preparing to participate in the Highland Games and getting the pub ready for taking part. In addition, they were providing mead for a stall at the event.

Graeme and Maisie were very excited.

Maisie probably more than Graeme. She'd set everything up and coordinated with the event organisers. She and Teagan were definitely the brains amongst the Baird brawn.

Murphy had woken up early. He'd spent the night at George's—something that was happening with increasing frequency. It made him smile whenever he was brought out of a deep sleep by a pug paw

to the face.

Life hadn't been lonely before, yet there had been a measure of it when the lights were out, and he'd been alone in his little flat above the brewery. Maybe it was because they'd known each other for so many years and been in an awkward crush phase for most of it. It felt like they were an old married couple who loved each other dearly.

That was the level of comfort they felt with one another.

"Are you ready?"

"Ready?" Murphy glanced back to find George had yet to open his eyes but was obviously awake.

"To fling heavy balls in my honour?" George rolled over on his side. He opened his eyes and smiled sleepily at him. "Are you ready?"

"I am always ready to fling heavy balls in your honour." Murphy managed a straight face for all of a second before they burst out laughing together. He groaned when his phone interrupted the moment. It took some scrambling for him to find it on the floor underneath his clothing. "What?"

"Morning, sunshine. Aren't you friendly this morning?"

"I am never friendly in the morning. What do you want, Evan?" Murphy gently eased Bumble over to George and got to his feet. He didn't want to be late for the game preparations. "Why are you even up this early?"

"Got a call from the delightfully cheerful Detective Constable Elwin Smith."

"Do you have a word quota to hit? We've known Elwin for years." Murphy grabbed his clothes off the floor, pausing to put the phone on speaker so George could listen to the conversation. He needed to head back to the brewery to grab his kilt and other kit for the sporting events he'd been taking part in later. "What's going on, Evan?"

"Marcello Lee has made a full confession. He apparently spoke to his barrister last night and decided to plead guilty. The police had found proof of his purchasing the venom. There was other evidence, but Elwin couldn't tell me more. Lee will go before the court next week to be sentenced for murder." Evan paused to take a breath. "All good news since it means none of you will be required to go to court. Thought you'd want to know."

"So you called me at six in the morning?"

"You were awake," Evan retorted defensively. "Shouldn't you have already skirted up for your day?"

"It's a kilt."

"Anyway, I'll be there cheering you on—or laughing when you fail." Evan hung up without a goodbye.

Murphy rubbed his eyes tiredly. He was reminded why he usually hated dealing with morning people. They were insufferably cheerful. "Did you hear?"

"Most of it." George sat up. He cuddled Bumble to his chest, resting his chin on top of the pug's head. "Think we'll ever really know why?"

"At the end of the day, I think greed is likely the answer. Not sure we'll ever get anything else. He's pled guilty unless he makes a statement to the court. After that, we'll never hear anything more." Murphy thought it was probably better to let the matter rest. "I've got to run. Meet me later?"

"We'll be there. I promised to help Margo keep my dad and yours at least somewhat under control." George flopped back onto the bed with a groan. "How on earth are we supposed to manage that? Remember three years ago?"

"When they decided to attempt hammer throwing, and both pulled muscles in their back? I'm fully aware." Murphy hadn't heard the end of it from his mother, who'd had to deal with a whining husband for days. "Let's hope they'll settle for a milder level of chaos."

"From your lips to their ears." George smiled when Murphy leaned over the bed to give him a kiss. "Off you go. I always enjoy seeing you in a kilt and vest."

With one last kiss, Murphy finished dressing and made his way out of the cottage. He noticed a moving van parked down the lane near the Griffin cottage. Hector's sister and boyfriend were finally packing everything up; he couldn't blame them for wanting to end the Dufftown chapter of their lives. They'd somehow managed a tentative truce, which was amusing all things considered.

Since Murphy was participating in one of the first events, he planned to skip out on the parade through the village. A few hours later, he could still hear the pipes and drums when they grew closer to the grounds set up for the Highland Games. As always, it sent a shiver up his spine and made him emotional.

The games in Dufftown stretched back hundreds of years. Murphy's family had been part of them for much of that history. He somehow always felt the weight of his ancestry with each beat of the drum. It was home.

It was family.

He paused with the weight ball in his hand. They all watched while the parade marched around the circuit. He'd be taking part in the tug-o'-war once the opening ceremony had finished.

In previous games, Murphy had entered multiple events but only joined a couple of the heavies this year. Graeme took part in the track ones but preferred to drink and sell mead. It was probably the wiser decision.

The weather had held right up until Murphy stepped up for his caber toss. Unfortunately, the clouds had chosen that exact moment to open up. He narrowly avoided the tree trunk slipping out of his grasp before he managed his run forward. It wasn't his best showing, but he was grateful not to have fallen on his arse like his brother had once done.

With his caber toss finished, Murphy trudged through the rain to find the brewery tent. He was soaking wet by the time he arrived. Graeme didn't appreciate it when he shook his head, sending water everywhere.

"You are not a dog. Stop it." Graeme tossed a towel in his direction. "Even if you currently smell like one."

"Ah, my son. My son." His dad came bounding

up in the rain. He ignored Graeme, who began complaining dramatically. "Of course, I have two boys, but only one tossed a caber."

While his father and brother playfully argued with each other, Murphy went in search of George. He found him hiding out under an umbrella with Bumble and Treacle. The two pups gave him an enthusiastic greeting.

"How'd you rank?"

"Somewhere above 'not the worst?'" Murphy hadn't honestly been paying much attention to how he'd done. He joined the games each year for the experience and the history, not necessarily to win. "Enjoying yourself?"

"More now." George took his hand, dragging him down into the chair Margo had vacated earlier. "Though, I do enjoy you in your kilt with your fancy socks."

"Stop teasing." Murphy gratefully accepted the bottle of water George handed to him. "Want to watch the dancing with me?"

"I just want to sit and relax. We can see the stage from here. It feels like for the first time in weeks that we've had a moment to catch our breath." George stretched his arm out to take Murphy's hand. "I was thinking about Hector Griffin and his boyfriend.

Would they have changed anything if they'd known time was short?"

"Maybe. It's always hard to say what someone might've done."

"Is it callous of me to say I've learnt something from his murder?"

"Not really. What have you learnt?" Murphy shifted his chair closer so the rain wasn't splashing on his legs.

"Life is very short. Too short, in fact, to not be a little brave."

"Oh?"

"We've known each other many years."

"We have."

"And been hopelessly in love with each other for quite a few of those years." George kept his gaze straight ahead as though his courage might fail him if he glanced at Murphy.

"We have," Murphy readily agreed. He couldn't help the wide grin slowly spreading across his face. There was something to be said for having those feelings fully out in the open. "We definitely have."

"My cottage has plenty of room for two. And it's not far from the brewery." George went on like he'd written a massive pros and cons list and wanted to share all the former. "It's nicer waking up with you than it is alone."

Murphy snorted in amusement. "Yes, I will move in with you."

"I haven't asked yet."

"Fair enough." Murphy exchanged a grin with him when George finally glanced in his direction. "Have you asked Bumble?"

"He gave an enthusiastic yes." George seemed relieved to have gotten this off his chest. "So, will you move in with us?"

"Of course, but only because Bumble agrees." Murphy saluted George with his bottle of water. "Here's to the future. May we have more sunshine and less murder."

BE on the lookout for book three, **HONEY MOON MURDER**. Looking for more MM cosy mysteries from Dahlia? Check out two fun series: **THE GRASMERE COTTAGE MYSTERY TRILOGY** and **LONDON PODCAST MYSTERY SERIES.**

ABOUT THE AUTHOR

Thanks for reading HONEY BEE MURDER. I do hope you enjoyed my story. I appreciate your help in spreading the word, including telling a friend. Before you go, it would mean so much to me if you would take a few minutes to write a review and share how you feel about my story so others may find my work. Reviews really do help readers find books. Please leave a review on your favorite book site.

Don't miss out on New Releases, Exclusive Giveaways, and much more!

Join my newsletter:

HTTP://EEPURL.COM/QONOX

Join my reader group:

WWW.FACEBOOK.COM/GROUPS/ 1108750876162947

I'd love to hear from you directly, too. Please feel free to email me at dahlia@dahliadonovan.com or check out my website HTTPS://DAHLIADONOVAN. COM/ for updates.

Dahlia Donovan wrote her first romance series after a crazy dream about shifters and damsels in distress. She prefers irreverent humour and unconventional characters. An autistic and occasional hermit, her life wouldn't be complete without her husband and her massive collection of books and video games.

facebook.com/dahliadonovan

twitter.com/DahliaDonovan

instagram.com/dahliadonovanauthor

pinterest.com/dahliadonovan

ACKNOWLEDGMENTS

A massive thank-you to my brilliant betas who take my first draft and help me turn it into something legible. To Becky, Olivia, and all the fantastic people at Tangled Tree and Hot Tree Publishing. And also to my beloved hubby, who keeps me from losing my mind while I'm stressing over word counts.

And, lastly, thank you, readers, for following me on my writing journey. I hope you enjoyed *Honey Bee Murder* and are looking forward to book three.

ABOUT THE PUBLISHER

Tangled Tree Publishing loves all things tangled and aims to bring darker, twisted, and more mind-boggling books to its readers. Publishing adult and new adult fiction, TTPubs are all about diverse reads in mystery, suspense, thrillers, and crime.

For more details, head to www. TANGLEDTREEPUBLISHING.COM

facebook.com/tangledtreepublishing

twitter.com/ttpubs

tiktok.com/@hottreepublishing